To Mrs. and Mr.
        Garnett,
Thank you for the
service and sacrifice to
our country. I hope you

TEARS OF SADNESS, TEARS OF JOY

enjoy this bit of history.

                Rhonda
                Harren
                June
                2004

D1715482

TEARS OF SADNESS, TEARS OF JOY

Rhonda S. Harrell

iUniverse, Inc.
New York Lincoln Shanghai

Tears of Sadness, Tears of Joy

iUniverse books may be ordered through booksellers or by contacting:

iUniverse
2021 Pine Lake Road, Suite 100
Lincoln, NE 68512
www.iuniverse.com
1-800-Authors (1-800-288-4677)

ISBN-13: 978-0-595-38121-0 (pbk)
ISBN-13: 978-0-595-82489-2 (ebk)
ISBN-10: 0-595-38121-9 (pbk)
ISBN-10: 0-595-82489-7 (ebk)

Printed in the United States of America

Acknowledgments

I, the author, Rhonda S. Higby Harrell would like to gratefully acknowledge the research of my husband, Charles T. Harrell. Wanting to support him in every way, including his obsessions, this book was written. I would also like to acknowledge another Harrell, Alfred Franklin III, whom we know as Frank. Frank is always supportive of my endeavors and helps emotionally and by being a good sounding board. You're my favorite big brother-in-law! I also acknowledge the help received from the book, The Eastern Shore of Virginia in Days Past, by Julie V. Nordstrom. Her pictures helped to inspire some of the places I have written about.

To Javan,
a Harrell and a Higby
of the highest caliber,
from Mom
August 2001

CHAPTER 1

▼

THE DISCOVERY

The late afternoon sun streamed in the old, tall window, highlighting the many dust particles floating in the air. The researcher looked tired, rubbing his eyes and setting aside the three books in front of him. "Surely the answer is out there, somewhere," he thought, as he smiled at the Star Trek sounding phrase and wondered how far "out there" might be.

Charles was not even directly descended from the man whom he was researching, but as a historian, he had to figure out what was fact and what was fiction for his own peace of mind. Alfred, his grandfather, had taken his father, Alfred Junior, to Delmar in 1929 to see the grave of his uncle, Samuel. The legend was that Samuel, a freight train engineer, had been killed in a derailment in 1913 caused by a man who wanted to ride the train but was kicked off by Samuel. The man had flipped the switch at a crossing just as the train was passing over it, causing it to crash into several cars parked on the siding. Sam had been killed in the incident.

Charles' father had taken him to the cemetery also, in 1972, and had taken his picture standing by the headstone. Thus the family legend was handed down. As Charles grew up he became interested in trains and modeling them, just like his father before him. Now, with a son of his own who shared the same interest, he recalled the story of Uncle Sam, related the incident to his son, wondered how much was fact and how much was fiction, and decided to find out.

Charles' son, Javan, was named for his great, great grandfather, who would have been Samuel's father. From what family history he knew, Javan and his wife, Ann Mitchell, had married in 1864, had ten children total, lived in the Nansemond County, Virginia area, worked as a farmer, married Defrosa McColter in 1910 after his first wife died, and himself died in 1924 in Suffolk, Virginia. One of those children was Samuel. He was the seventh of ten children to be born to his parents, but two, Sue and Charles Lee, had died in infancy. That much was fact. Charles had seen the census records and birth, death, and marriage certificates to verify everything. He didn't trust oral history, knowing how messed up a story can become while traveling from one person to the next. But what about the train accident? Why was he having such trouble finding any information about that?

To stretch his legs and clear his mind, he decided to go to the Archives. Maybe an article would be written about the accident in a local newspaper. So he returned the books he had been looking through, gathered his supplies, and checked out through the metal detectors and security devices.

Engrossed in thought during the short walk, he hardly noticed the buildings or people around him. Having grown up in the Washington, D.C. area, he felt perfectly comfortable around large cities, not fearing the people or place as many outsiders did.

Once inside, he found himself a seat and requested The New York Times for the week of March 8, 1913. So many railroads went through Delmar. Which one did Sam work for? Was he in Delaware at the time? Or was it Maryland, Pennsylvania, or Virginia? Too many questions bounced around in his mind.

"Calm down," he thought to himself, "and be systematic."

One step at a time was the best approach. Which train would be most likely? After an hour of skimming through newspaper articles, Charles needed a break. He got up and stretched. Maybe requesting a different newspaper would help. So he went back, requested the Baltimore Sun, then got his drink of water while he waited.

"Nothing," he kept thinking. This wasn't like his usual genealogical researches that seemed to come easily to him because of his logical mind, great knowledge of history, and familiarity with the Archives and libraries.

"This is going to take a miracle," he thought as he sat back down and promised his tired eyes that he'd work for only an hour more.

Then, there it was. Without even turning a page, the article on the bottom of the right hand column entitled "Two Killed in Collision, Fast Freight Runs Into Open Switch Near Cape Charles" literally jumped out at him. According to the article, Uncle Sam "was killed and the fireman, Virgil H. Hearn was fatally injured at 4:25 on the morning of March 19, 1913 when their fast freight train on the New York, Philadelphia and Norfolk railroad ran into an open switch at Bellehaven Station. The injured man died several hours later in the Norfolk Hospital where he was taken for treatment. Both men lived at Delmar, Del. The engineer dashed into a switch, upon which were six cars loaded with cinders. The engine and five cars were demolished and eight others derailed. The lock to the switch was broken and thrown away, and the railroad officials express the belief that it was a deliberate attempt to wreck the train."

Charles hastily wrote the name of the paper, the date, and the page number in his notes. Then he went to get a photocopy of the document. It confirmed that such an accident had occurred, and the name of the railroad was stated. Now that was a real find! With that information, he could go back in company records and discover more facts. Gathering his things, he headed for home with a lighter step and a sense of rightness with the world.

After dining with his family that evening and relating his day's successes, he sat down at the computer to enter the information as he had it. Later he showered and went to bed. How did it get to be 1:30 already? Well, the family was all asleep, so he quietly slipped into bed and turned off the light.

CHAPTER 2

▼

THE MEETING

The day dawned bright and beautiful, with a fresh breeze from the east keeping it cool for now. As Sam made his way out to the train yard, he thought about what this day, June 3, meant to him. This was the day that his precious daughter was born...then died, and his sweet Virdie along with her. It was supposed to be the happiest day of this life, but it turned out to be the saddest. He wanted in some way to keep her face imprinted in his memory and to treasure what they had together. He wanted to place flowers on her grave, at least, but he was miles away.

He and Vicky had married in Nansemond County, Virginia. She was so beautiful, so young, and so much better off in social standing than he. But it had been one of those "once in a lifetime" love affairs, or so he thought then.

His family tried their hand at whatever came along, mostly farming and fishing on the great expanse of water around his native Nansemond County. The ocean wasn't far away, and the bay and inlets always provided oysters and eels that could be sold up north at a pretty price. So, for a while, his family had done well, by their standards. But Vicky came from a different world.

Her uncle's family lived in the Georgian two story brick home across the inlet from his small cottage at Drivers. Their plantation was called Sunbury, an appropriate name for a place where the sun shone brightly and living off the land was easy. They had hired help that stayed on all the time. They farmed 160 acres, had livestock, and her uncle was an insurance salesman in the city of Suffolk. They were used to wealth and easy living. He was used to work. And that was how they met.

Her uncle's family consisted of himself, his wife Verna, and four daughters, Elizabeth, Sarah, Mary, and Margaret. The girls were doted on and given everything they wished. Although their father never said that he wished he had boys to help out on the farm, he often had to hire workers to help, especially at planting and harvest times. Like Javan's grandfather, Jesse, the Brittanhaur family had freed their slaves long prior to the Civil War. Many had made that personal decision, but many of the blacks had stayed on the plantations as freed men, not knowing where else to go and sometimes because the families were truly close to each other, with a fondness and affection that comes only from living through good and bad times together. That was why "Uncle Elliot" lived in a little cabin on the western edge of the plantation. He was a beloved member of the family, but had a place of his own.

Several servants helped Verna around the house, but their tasks consisted of cleaning, cooking, sewing, maintaining the kitchen garden, and putting up the produce thereof. They felt fondly toward the Brittanhaur family for whom they worked because they were always treated well, but Arthur was careful to take care of them, consider their feelings, and not over-work them. Arthur also felt that although his daughters couldn't and shouldn't help in the fields or with the livestock, they were not above helping out with little chores around the house. One of the tasks they performed was carrying water and small treats to the hired hands during planting and harvesting time. Arthur felt that workers who were well cared for and happy were more likely to do a better job. To be respectful and "proper," the girls always had to go to the field in pairs, but they knew and understood their father's philosophies toward people, no matter what their station in life.

Javan and his family, on the other hand, needed to think about today and the future. Making a living for a large family without benefit of a substantial plantation and the means to work it was hard. So Javan and his boys had turned to fishing. The area folk said the bay had been fished out. The catch each day was barely enough to feed the family. So one day Sam took a boat, rowed across the river, and walked boldly up to the imposing house and requested work. Fortunately, it was harvest time and extra help was needed. He worked hard that fall, bringing in the peanut and cotton crop alongside other hired hands of both black and white coloring. But he was noticed by the foreman. He worked hard, he was always cheerful, and he would volunteer to do more if that was what was needed. He never shirked hard work.

It wasn't long before others took notice of him, too. The beautiful niece, Victoria, would bring water to the fields around mid-morning and mid-afternoon along with her cousin, Sarah. To Sarah, it was a routine chore, but to Victoria it was an adventure. She was from New York City and had come to attend Elizabeth's wedding, which took place the first Saturday after she arrived. During this trip she also had an extended stay while her family sold their house and prepared to move to a larger, more elaborate one on the east side. Her uncle didn't mind her coming, for he teased "If I'm going to lose one girl, it'd be nice to fill the gap with another." He always teased her fondly in such a way that she invariably felt comfortable there.

Victoria was used to having servants around, but they were different from these hired hands. Her servants were always immaculately dressed and immaculately polite. These men were rough in every way, and they sometimes worked in the sun bare-chested, which she had never seen before. The odors of the bay, the peanuts, and the men's sweat all combined to make the fields a fairy tale adventure for her.

Nothing had prepared her for what she was about to encounter on this warm September day, hauling water to the fields with her cousin. She saw a shock of flaming red hair that the work in the sun had made even more prominent. She noticed his large frame and broad shoulders. His tanned arms and strong legs caught her eye as she watched from a respectable distance as the hired hands finished coming down a row to where the two girls were. It was easy to spot him with that flaming hair.

"Good morning, Miss Sarah, Ma'am," he said, "and thank you for the water."

After several days of hauling water to the fields around mid-morning and again mid-afternoon, her cousin Sarah grew tired of the chore. "It just isn't fittin' work for a lady," she would complain. So Victoria offered to do it herself today. It wasn't as hot as it had been, and the men wouldn't need as much, so she knew she could handle two buckets by herself. Sarah, content to stay in the shade of the looming magnolia trees near the house, picked up her needlework and replied, "Thank you ever so much, cousin Victoria. I just don't feel up to the exercise today."

So Victoria filled the two buckets at the well and headed off toward the field. She knew it wasn't much, but the men always seemed so thankful for that bit of water and a moment to rest. "You're welcome." she would always reply as each man carefully took a scoopful of the water from the bucket. Some drank it and some poured it over their heads, but each was careful to take only one scoop so that they all had some. Then it was back to work.

This morning she was feeling particularly bold. As Sam's turn came at the bucket, he said, "Thank you for the water, Miss Victoria."

Surprised, she inquired of him, "How do you know my name?"

He smiled a flash of even, white teeth. "I've heard the foreman say 'Here comes Miss Sarah and Miss Victoria with the water bucket.' I know Miss Sarah is the master's daughter, so I assumed that your name is Miss Victoria. It is your name, isn't it?"

"Well, yes," she replied, hesitating as she blushed.

"I'm sorry. Maybe I was too informal. Would you rather I call you something else?"

"My friends call me Vicky," she replied, surprised to hear herself say that.

"Then may I be so fortunate as to be considered your friend?" he asked gently, almost under his breath.

Caught up in the moment, she replied, "Yes, I'd like that."

Just then the foreman blew his whistle and it was back to the field for Sam. He smiled as he walked away, and Victoria just stood there, pondering what had just happened between them.

For the next four days her cousin Sarah feigned faintness and shortness of breath as an excuse to not haul water to the fields. But Victoria didn't mind. In fact, she looked forward to that time of day. The rest of the hours on the huge plantation seemed to drag along, but her heart jumped and her breath came shorter when she walked with anticipation of seeing that red hair and those prominent freckles again. Even Sarah noticed the change in her and commented on it, "Why, Cousin Victoria, dear. It seems that you like to take water to the hired men," she would say, her voice tinted with disgust.

"Oh, Sarah, it's just so different from New York. The novelty of it, you know," she would reply and hope that her mixed emotions weren't making her sound totally daft. But Sarah didn't notice. As long as she didn't have to go, she was content.

If Victoria's parents ever dreamed that her heart had become stolen by a common laborer in Virginia, they would ban her from ever visiting there again, she was sure. In fact, she had received their letter yesterday. It stated that the house was nearly finished and that she would be leaving in just a few days. Upon her return, they planned to throw one of the most elaborate parties the East Side had ever seen. She knew, of course, that it was a "coming out" party. Her parents would invite all the eligible bachelors of the high society of New York, hoping for at least one suitable match for her. They were from the "old school" and greatly anticipated that their only daughter would marry well, have children, and would be content to manage a household that consisted of servants, dinner parties, and afternoon teas with the society ladies. In her mother's eyes, she could ask no more from life.

Up until a few weeks ago, she had dreamed the same dream. Rich clothes, dainty foods, and the latest hair fashions had dominated her interests. Even her mother's manner of showing off by having all the latest gadgets had seemed exciting to her before. She had looked forward to seeing the new kitchen with linoleum, the telephone, and the electric lights and heating in every room. Now all that seemed frivolous. Was her mother that superficial? Was she?

How would her mother respond to her having a romantic interest in Virginia? Especially one who was not from the upper crust? Dare she even tell her mother about this? Maybe, if it came up in the conversation. She would claim an intellectual interest in how other people lived and a Christian concern in wanting to help the less fortunate. But, to be honest with herself, she knew it was more than that. She knew she was attracted to this bronzed Atlas and wanted to know more about him, his life, and his family.

Three days later, Sarah was back to helping again. Victoria wasn't sure this was a good thing because now she felt that she needed to portray a respectable attitude and treat the men as Sarah did. But she had really preferred the playful banter of the previous few days when she had come with her cousin Margaret, who was younger and noticed a lot less than Sarah. Now that Victoria's time here was almost at an end, she really wanted one more time alone, a time to speak to Sam, to say good-bye. The morning passed uneventfully.

That afternoon, her Aunt Verna was over-seeing the finishing touches on a new dress for Sarah. The family was throwing a going away party for Victoria that night. It was to be quite a social event for them. Uncle had invited many townspeople, had hired a band, and had even approved of new dresses for all the women folk of the family. Victoria's was already made and fitted, so she seized the opportunity to take the water to the fields with Margaret again while Sarah was being pushed here and pulled there and had pins and needles flying around her.

Happy that an excuse had presented itself, her feet fairly flew down the path toward the peanut field nearest the river. Getting there a little early, she stood and looked across, wondering what life was like on the other side. She knew there was another large plantation, for she could see its gleaming rooftops. But that didn't hold her interest nearly as much as trying to figure out where Sam lived. She strained her eyes to spot some small cottage, but couldn't see anything for the lush foliage. She was concentrating so hard that she didn't notice the men working their way toward her for a drink of water.

"Miss?" the foreman broke into her reverie as he took his turn at the bucket first, "Is everything alright?"

"Oh, good afternoon, yes, thank you." The words stumbled out of her mouth as she tried to regain her composure and collect her thoughts. "I am to leave tomorrow and I was just thinking about how much I will miss this area."

The men filed past the bucket silently, each one thinking his own thoughts. Sam purposefully waited till last. When he had the chance, he quietly spoke to her. "Is it true? You're leaving tomorrow?"

"Yes, Sam," she replied sadly. "I hate to go, but our house is finished in New York and I have to go home."

Boldly, knowing that he wouldn't get another chance, Sam asked, "Then may I write you there?"

"No!" she said, almost a little too loudly. To not draw attention, she lowered her voice but kept her eyes fixed on his. "My parents would never permit me to return to Virginia if they thought I…well…" She blushed for a moment at the unspoken words on her mind, then went on knowing that their time together was short. "And I do so want to come back as soon as I can."

"Then let me take you on a boat ride. Tonight. After dark."

Her mind raced. Could she sneak out of the house during the party? No. That was impossible.

"Uncle is throwing a party in my honor tonight. I have to be there. Who knows how long that will last. I just don't see how I can manage it."

Sam, unwilling to give up so easily, said, "I will wait. I will wait on my dock right across the way. When the party is over and you think everyone has gone asleep, sneak out. Take a lantern but don't light it till you get to this spot. I will see you from my dock and will row over to get you. It will take about 10 minutes, so just wait for me here. OK?"

The foreman blew his whistle just then. Without time to think it through in her head, her heart said, "Yes. I'll be here."

Some of the men hurried over to say good-bye and thank you as they headed back toward the field. Several shook her hand and she noticed the roughness and firmness of their grasp. She marveled that these men were so kind in their hearts when their skin was so rough and she thought about the soft handed gentlemen she knew at home. She chuckled to herself as she thought of her pastor's weekly handshake, something akin to shaking a day old fish compared to this.

The rest of the day went by in a flurry of activity with getting ready for the party and the party itself. The servants had rolled the carpets from the huge parlor, the band played in one corner, and many elegant couples waltzed around the floor. Victoria found herself standing by the refreshment table alone for a moment. She had danced with practically every young man in the room, but none of them seemed to be in the least bit interesting. It was true that they would talk in generalities, but she noticed that most of them preferred to talk about themselves. Their jobs, their families, their this, that and the other consumed them. She would have enjoyed someone asking her about her life, her hopes, and her dreams. But she imagined that they all assumed hers were the same as every other girl her age: get married, have children, manage the household, host parties, etc. She glanced at her watch and noticed that it read 11:15 already. "Oh, my," she gasped to herself, realizing that she had enjoyed the evening. Her uncle, overhearing her gasp as he came toward her for a dance, asked, "Is something wrong, my dear?"

"Oh, no, Uncle, of course not." She replied. "It is a perfectly beautiful evening. I was just amazed at how quickly the time has gone." She felt she had made the recovery well.

"Are you getting tired? You do have a big journey ahead of you tomorrow."

Seeing this as her opportunity to bring things to a close here, she sighed and said, "Well, yes, I guess I am getting somewhat tired."

"Then that's it." Her uncle clapped his hands several times to get everyone's attention, made a brief speech that thanked everyone for coming to the party, then said this would be the last dance of the evening. Thankfully, he insisted on dancing it with her, so she didn't have to choose between the several gentlemen who had headed her way.

"I believe you've made quite an impression on some of the men of Virginia," he grinned as he whirled her around the room.

"Thank you, Uncle. You have been so kind to me during my stay. I sincerely hope I have made a good impression on your friends and that I will be welcome here again soon," she purred. Her uncle, always doting on the women folk of the house, gave them every whim they ever had. But he could afford to, and he enjoyed their fancies.

"Yes, yes, any time you wish," he said as he waltzed with her, surprisingly fleet footed for a gentleman of his age, "Any time."

To Victoria it seemed that it took an eternity for the household to settle down. She had easily excused herself to her room with the reason that she needed plenty of rest before her long journey home. Then her cousins all retired, along with her uncle and aunt, but the household servants then had to tidy up and put away the food. She lay in her bed, waiting, and doing her best not to fall asleep. Finally, when all was quiet, she slid out of bed, put on her slippers, and went down the back stairs. She could hear the sound of heavy breathing come from her aunt and uncle's room. After getting down the stairs, she was confident she could get the rest of the way to the beach with no problem. If she did run across some servant, she could use the excuse of needing to use the out building. But they shouldn't question her.

Her feet fairly flew along the path she had traveled so many times to the fields, then down to the water's edge. She noticed that her feet were wet, probably with the dew that lay so heavy in this area and the fact that she still had on just her slippers. They were quieter than her regular boots, plus she didn't need to spoil the shine that had so carefully been put on them for the party and her going away. Her aunt and uncle had taken great pains to be sure she went back to New York in as good of shape as she came. Everything, including her bags, had been cleaned and polished that day. But, those thoughts were far from her mind as she quickly lit a lucifer against a rock and lit the lantern she had been careful to leave in her room that night. Then, she waited.

She could hear the gentle waves lapping against the shore and wondered how many boats were out there. She wondered if Sam had seen her signal and where they would row to. It didn't matter, she reasoned, as long as she had some time to talk to him alone. Surprised at her own brazenness, she shivered with a fleeting thought of what her uncle would do if he ever found out she had sneaked out of the house to meet a common farm hand at this hour of the night.

Then he was there. Magically appearing, he slid his rowboat beside her and clambered out as easily as if he had done this all his life.

"Hello, Vicky," he said and seemed to pause, not knowing what to say next.

"Good evening, Sam. Thank you for waiting for me. I'm ready for my ride in your boat."

So Sam obediently stepped aside and offered her his hand as she entered the boat. Then he pushed off from shore and jumped in himself. She noticed again how rough his hand was, but how gentlemanly he treated her.

"Where would you like to go?" he asked in a voice as quiet and soothing as the waves.

"How about to your house?" she offered.

"No, my folks are asleep and it wouldn't do well to arouse them. But I'll show you our dock and where we usually fish."

As he rowed, she watched the muscles in his arms and chest ripple beneath the light shirt he wore. The temperature was less than the dew point, but the exertion of rowing kept him warm. He seemed to suddenly notice that she might be chilled, so he offered her a blanket that he kept in the bottom of the boat. She gratefully wrapped it around her shoulders then started to ask questions in a low voice.

"Can you tell me about your family?"

She seemed truly interested, and he found himself telling her all about his family moving from place to place, trying their hand at anything to make some money. The Civil War had been part of the family's downfall. His father, Javan, had been wounded. Although it wasn't a fatal wound, it seemed to kill his spirit. After the war was over, the family noticed that he had changed; he had trouble settling down to anything. He had tried working as a farmer, a fisherman, a carpenter, a mason, and everything in between. Sam told her how he had not been able to finish his schooling as he hoped because his help was needed to earn money for the family. With younger brothers in the family, it was part of his responsibility to see they had plenty of food and shoes on their feet.

He told her how his older brother Robert was a fairly successful farmer. He and his wife Lizzie had four children and even had a servant living in their house. Sam seemed very proud of that fact and that both of them could read and write.

Then, he said, came Richard. There were other babies in between, but they had died in infancy. Richard, he told her, was a lumber inspector. He was renting a house in Surry County, but Sam noted that he and his wife, Mary Ann, could not read or write. They had two children, but one had recently died.

Victoria was amazed that he so openly talked of the death of infants. To him, it was just a part of life and seemed expected. She had never known anyone who had a child die, so she made a point in her mind to ask her mother about how frequently that happened and why.

Next he told her about Charles Edward. The family called him Charlie, but people in the area called him "Captain Charlie" because he worked with his father-in-law, Joseph Etheridge, as a fisherman and seemed to prosper at it. He, according to Sam, had tried his hand at farming also, but couldn't make a go of it. Sam told her that some people just had a knack for knowing when to plant and when to reap, but Charlie wasn't one of them. To him, it seemed like a mystery. But fishing, on the other hand, came as natural as falling out of a tree. He loved the water and everything about it. Sam told her that Charlie and his wife, Julia, had lost a child already, but did have one son living.

His sister Rosa was next in line. She had married Joseph Hubbard only six months prior. They didn't have any children yet, but he suspected he would be an uncle again soon. Her husband worked as a special agent for the New York, Philadelphia, and Norfolk railroad. Sam admitted that he had never ridden a train, but that it was something that he thought he would like to do very much.

He came next in line, then after him were three more brothers, all at home yet. James came next and he was generally in poor health. His doctor bills kept the family strapped for cash quite often. After him were Walter and then Ben. Sam said that those last two were as inseparable as could be. They were always together and always watching out for each other, almost like twins. Sam told how they even played jokes on other family members together and stuck up for each other. He commented that he wouldn't be surprised if they married sisters some day or worked together somehow.

Sam noted that he and his brother Walt worked for her uncle now and enjoyed it a lot, but it kept them both from attending any school. Sam himself was born in 1881, so he had just turned 17. He said he had missed several years of schooling due to working, but would love to go back to school, even if he were the oldest and tallest in the building.

His brother Walt, he told her, was 16. He had to work, too, but didn't seem to mind so much. He was an outdoors man from the very start. Sam related an incident from his childhood about when the family couldn't find Walt for the longest time. Finally they looked up to heaven for help, and there he was, sound asleep in a tree. Ben was always hunting or fishing, Sam commented with some admiration, for it brought in extra food for the family.

Sam also mentioned that Ben, at age 14, got to go to school simply because his mother insisted. The rest of the boys didn't mind, but sometimes his Dad got put out with it, he said. In the meantime, Ben was good about sharing new knowledge and books with his older brothers. Usually they were tired from a long day's work, but there was always a little quiet time in front of the fire before going to bed when Ben would share his day's adventures. Sam said that he and Walt both were glad of it. It kept them up on their learning and seemed to keep the family close.

Victoria was amazed at this. In her family, where money was never a problem, she had taken education for granted. In fact, she was rather dreading going back to New York and starting her classes again. In contrast, Sam told her, he read everything he could get his hands on. As he put it, his family might have him down for now, but they couldn't keep him down.

He was hesitant to tell her that he had a knack for learning mechanical things. He liked to work with machines and was able to repair most anything. That, at his home, was a necessity, as buying new things was out of the question. But he hoped his aptitude would be able to land him a good job some time. He told her he dreamed about leaving the Drivers area and living some place exciting and having enough money in his pocket to buy a soda whenever he wished.

She chuckled a little at the simplicity of his dream, but then turned serious when he asked her what she dreamed of doing in life. As she tried to explain to him how high class society worked in New York, he interrupted her, and repeated the question.

"But, what do you dream of doing with your life? What do you really want to do and be five or ten years from now?"

The question unnerved her. It was as if she had never really thought about it before. She had never allowed herself to dream beyond what was expected of her. So she quietly said, "I don't know. In my world there's a big difference between what a girl dreams of doing and what a girl gets to do."

"It ought to be one and the same," Sam replied. "If it is for me, it ought to be for you."

The two of them rowed around for a little while more with Sam pointing out favorite spots of his: the place where the family's fishing nets were, where he had capsized an old row boat when he was ten but managed to come out of it alive, and his favorite thinking spot.

Suddenly, Victoria realized that he still fished. "Do you mean you work at Uncle's farm all day long and then fish in the night, too?"

"Of course," he said, "The money I make has gone toward clothes and shoes for the family and James' doctor bills. Now I'm saving up a little for some new books and for the winter. We don't spend money on food. If we can't grow it or catch it or hunt it, we don't eat it."

This was another revelation to her and it boggled her mind. Then, again, another realization came to her. "Then you haven't slept at all yet tonight and you have to work on the farm all day tomorrow."

"Yes, that's true, but it's OK," he answered with a smile that she thought would melt even her mother's heart. "I might be a little tired tomorrow, but I would rather be a little tired and get the chance to know you a little better than to get enough sleep and never take that chance."

She was amazed at his forthrightness and sacrifice for her. "Then I must let you go. Besides, I need to get back into the house before the kitchen staff starts making breakfast."

He agreed and rowed her back toward her uncle's farm where she had met him. "Vicky?" he started, "may I write you?"

She thought for a moment, arguing in her heart and mind. Finally, she answered him in as straight forward a manner as he talked with her. "I would cherish every letter, Sam, but if my parents found out, they would never let me come back here again. As it is, I feel confident that they will let me return for a rest over Spring Break. Can I count on seeing you again when I return?"

Sam seemed a little downcast for a moment, then said with a sincerity in his voice that made her heart ache that the answer couldn't have been different, "Yes, I suppose that is best. I will be here when you return, and I will count the minutes till then."

He rowed up against the shore, deftly jumped out and made the boat secure, then offered her his hand again. She got up a little stiffly from dancing so much that evening and sitting still for so long. "Good night, then, Sam, and thank you."

"Good night, Vicky." He watched as she went safely up the bank, then he quickly disappeared into the darkness that covered the water.

Victoria was able to sneak back into the house and her room easily enough, but finding sleep was another matter. She lay there in her luxurious feather bed and wondered about what had just happened to her. She seemed to be in another world, and she was uncertain as to whether or not she liked it. The more she thought about it, the more confused she became. "Oh, well," she thought in her typical level-headed way, "I'm sure it will all be clear with the morning sun." Then she must have dozed off, but it seemed only moments till her aunt called for her to get up and get ready for the big day that would see her traveling 200 miles north of this place that held so many fond memories for her.

CHAPTER 3

▼

THE EXPECTATION

As she had expected, Victoria had attended party after party upon her return to New York. Her mother, who was from the social elite of that city, refused to believe that her daughter, of all people, couldn't find a suitable match in a city that size. The subject had become a source of contention between the two of them and the subject of Sam had never conveniently arisen.

"Mother," Victoria started one morning, "I would very much like to go visit Uncle Arthur and Aunt Verna over Spring Break. May I please?"

"Now, Victoria, really. You know there are going to be several parties to attend during that week. To tell you the truth, I really don't see what interest you have in that dreary place. It is always muggy and hot. It simply spoils a new hair do and makes my dresses feel so sticky. I don't know how your father stood it all those years growing up there."

Having said her piece, her mother busied herself with the morning routine of looking through the mail, skimming the newspaper, and ordering servants around.

Victoria tried again, from a different angle. "Mother, you know that cousin Sarah turns 16 in a few weeks. I'm sure Uncle Arthur will be giving a party in her honor. I wouldn't want to miss it. You know Cousin Sarah came clear up here for my 16th coming out party. Shouldn't we reciprocate?"

Her mother looked at her, smiled, and said, "Perhaps you have more social awareness than I gave you credit for. You're right. I will make the arrangements for your traveling today. You can take the train as far as the house in Cape Charles, take the ferry across, and take a carriage from there. Agreed?"

"Oh, thank you, Mother," Victoria sighed and gave her mother a hug. "I've got to go now and plan which dresses I will take."

She whirled out of the room, obviously excited about the prospect. Her mother smiled to herself and tried to remember what it was like to be nearly 17. Perhaps, she thought, her daughter would turn out to be acceptable after all.

Cape Charles began as a railroad town in the 1880's, so most of the houses were no more than ten years old. Victoria's parents used their house there as a place to take important guests who preferred peace to the social hubbub of the city. Her father often took important clients, as he did on this trip. As a resort and refuge for the wealthy of New York, Victoria often saw her friends here and didn't see that coming here was too much different from staying in the city. But to her father, anything that brought him that much closer to his beloved Virginia and the ocean was worth any price.

As it turned out, Victoria's Uncle Arthur was a close, personal friend of her father's client. So her father, the client, Victoria, and several servants traveled on the train south together as far as their Victorian home in Cape Charles. Her Uncle Arthur, anxious to see his brother after several years, took the ferry across the bay the day after they arrived. It was a congenial meeting of friends and family. As far as her father was concerned, this was a superb trip. His wife, who could sometimes be too pushy with concerns about "etiquette," had stayed in New York. So after his client left, closing a tremendous deal while there, he and his brother had a few days to chat and catch up on old times. They compared notes about old acquaintances and caught each other up on family news. They laughed, walked along the beach, and thoroughly enjoyed each other's company. At the end of the two days, her father saw her and her uncle to the ferry.

Shaking hands, he said, "Take good care of her, Arthur. You know she's a ray of sunshine in my life."

Feeling similarly, Arthur replied, "Now, William, you know how I feel about girls. Be sure that I'll do my best." With that, Victoria gave her father a kiss on the cheek good-bye and boarded the ferry that would take her back to the mansion on the river that held her heart.

Victoria spent her first day at Sunbury with her family. Her Aunt Verna was in a flurry making arrangements for Cousin Sarah's birthday party. This was truly her element, to order here, plan there, arrange this, and re-arrange that. Victoria was so anxious to get out to the fields that she could hardly contain her excitement, but knew she needed to show an interest in her family and her reason for being here. So she tried to be as helpful as she could. By late afternoon, she couldn't take any more.

"Auntie, I feel so cooped up after being on the beach for a few days. May I please have your permission to go for a walk?"

Aunt Verna raised her eyebrows. "By yourself?"

Victoria paused a moment, not knowing how to answer that question without being obvious. "Well, I know you are all busy with the planning and things and I couldn't ask you to take time out just to walk with me, so, yes, by myself would be alright."

"Alright, then, go if you must, but please keep clean and be back before sunset."

"Thank you, Auntie, you're the best." With a quick kiss on her aunt's cheek, she donned her hat and gloves and was out the door.

"Thank God you girls don't have that wild streak in you," her aunt sighed after her, to nobody in particular. Her female cousins didn't reply.

As Victoria tried to maintain a calm walk toward the fields, her heart raced ahead of her. A hundred questions jumbled through her head, such as "Was he there? Would he remember her? Would they be able to plan to get together?"

When she arrived at the field nearest the river, she saw the foreman. Her heart jumped and she scanned the rows of cotton being planted. No red hair.

The foreman came up to her and spoke kindly, "Well, if it isn't Miss Victoria. What are you doing here, child? These boys don't need any water yet!"

Fearing that she looked very foolish, she tried to calmly say, "I just arrived today and I was curious to see how the fields had changed since last fall. The rest of the family is so busy with plans for Cousin Sarah's birthday party that I decided to get out of the way and go for a walk for a while."

Her speech must have seemed convincing enough, for the foreman continued the conversation, thinking she had a real interest in the planting of cotton. "Well, the fields look a lot different now than they do in September and October. If you thought picking cotton was hard work, look at this. Every seed has to be planted by hand. These boys have to stoop over and then measure out with their foot where the next seed will go. They have to be exactly 18 inches apart to give the mature plant enough room to grow." He went on some more in that vein, while Victoria wondered how to get the information she longed for. Finally, it came to her.

"There seem to be fewer men in the field than there were last fall. Why is that?"

"You have a very observant eye, child. Yes, we are several hands short. Poor old Uncle Elliot died during the winter. He was old and his time had come. One young man, named Gilbert, decided to take a job in town. I guess he had some connections somewhere. He works at a hotel, from what I hear. And that red-headed boy who was always so hard-working still is on the farm. You know how generous to a fault your uncle is. Well, after Elliot died, he offered his cabin on the west end of the plantation to Sam and his family. You see, one of Sam's brothers had just gotten married and not only that, Sam, his brother Walt, and his father were all working for us by that time. I forget when you left. Was that before they all started working here? I'll bet it was. Yes, they are all good workers. So your uncle decided to keep them on all winter. Well, we had such a harsh winter that sometimes they couldn't get across the river in their boat because the water froze up almost solid across. So, like I said, after Elliot died, we offered them the cabin, and they gladly took it. The lady cleaned it up and it looks real nice, now. And all three of them are handy, in more ways than one. Your uncle gave them 10 acres to work on the west end of Sunbury. It hasn't been anything but underbrush before. I don't know what the whole deal is, but I suspect they can keep part of the profits off the land for themselves in exchange for clearing the land and working it. Also, they are on call. Anytime I need them for work in these fields, all I got to do is call on them. And if anything breaks down around here, I can call on them to fix it. They are all three some of the handiest people you'd ever hope to meet."

Victoria was surprised about such a long monologue from the foreman. Usually he was a business only sort of man, but she must have caught him on a good day today. Just at that moment the men started coming out of the rows near them, so he said, "Well, I've got to get these men started back down the right rows. So duty calls. Nice seeing you again, Miss Victoria."

Being aptly dismissed, she replied, "Thank you. I'll see you again soon."

She swished away with her heart leaping in her chest again and her brain racing on ahead of her. How could she get to the west end of the plantation without letting on her intentions? That was an obstacle she would have to overcome, but not today. She noticed the pink glow in the west and hurried back to the mansion with thoughts pouring through her of how proud she was that Sam and his family had distinguished themselves on the plantation.

As it turned out, Victoria needn't have worried herself over how to get to the western edge of the plantation to see Sam. He was well known around the place as a man who could fix anything mechanical, and while the preparations for the party were having finishing touches on them, the pump in the kitchen broke. Uncle Arthur was proud of having one of the first ones in the area. With a cistern under the kitchen area, all anyone had to do was pump the water up into the kitchen. It was a welcome addition from having to go out to the well for any.

So Sam was called in to fix the pump, as water was necessary for cleaning and getting ready for the great party. But Victoria didn't know he had been summoned. She, wanting to appear helpful while trying to figure out her own dilemma, offered to help her female cousins bathe and get ready for the party. So she had just come down the back stairs with an empty bucket when she looked up to see Sam standing directly in front of her.

She stopped short, "Oh, I…" she started but couldn't find any words to go on.

Sam, with his usual jolliness, jumped up off the floor from where he had been working, wiped his hands on his pants, and exclaimed in a voice a bit high in pitch and volume, "Miss Victoria! I didn't know you were here!"

Victoria noted the sound of surprise and delight in his voice, then finding hers, was able to explain. "Yes, I just came in this morning with Uncle. I couldn't miss Cousin Sarah's 16th birthday party, you know, and…" her voice dropped to almost a whisper as she looked around quickly to see if anyone was within ear shot, "I promised you I'd be back in the Spring, Sam."

His eyes lowered and so did his voice, "Yes, I've thought about you a lot since last September and wondered if you would keep your word."

She also noticed that his ruddy skin seemed even more so and she wondered if he were blushing. Trying to cover their conversation and make him feel more comfortable, she said, "I hear everyone is really impressed with the way you work and you live on the western edge of the plantation now. Congratulations. I'm real proud of you, Sam."

He looked her straight in the eyes now and she noticed how blue his eyes were compared to hers. "Thank you, Vicky. That means a lot to me. I'm trying to save up some money and make something of myself. I have reason to now."

Not noticing the hidden meaning, Victoria went on talking, "Oh, Sam, I always thought you would make good. You have such an interest in reading and learning. I admire that. I must admit I have done better in my studies this year because of what you'd said about learning while we were out in the…"

At that point her sentence cut short as they both heard footsteps coming down the stairs behind her. She looked up to see two of her female cousins coming, asking "Now, Victoria, where is that water? We can't get ready for a party without a bath first. Oh, hi, Sam."

They didn't seem to think it was odd at all for him to be in the house.

"Ladies, I'm sorry. I'm going to need just a few minutes to get this new-fangled pump fixed and then you can have all the water you need. I hope waiting won't make you late for the party."

Margaret and Mary giggled and said, "We like to be late for parties. Fashionably late entrances make for grand entrances!"

Sam said nothing as he went to work, but Victoria was sure he was thinking that he wouldn't know about such things. In a matter of minutes he tested the pump, primed it with some water left over at the sink from the washing of dishes, and it flowed perfectly.

"Sam, you're a miracle worker," Mary commented. "Thanks ever so much."

She drew some water then went on upstairs. The other cousin followed her with another bucket. "I'll be up in just a moment," Victoria called after them. "When can I see you again...so we can talk some more?" she asked Sam hesitatingly, not wanting to seem too forward.

"Tomorrow is Sunday," he started. "How about in the afternoon, after church? Do you think you can get away?"

"Yes. That's a great idea!" Victoria agreed. "Come by here and I'll be sure to be ready." She filled her bucket and went up the stairs with a lightness in her heart and step that she hadn't felt for a long time.

Uncle Arthur was insistent on his rule that if you could party on a Saturday night, you could also get up and go to church on Sunday morning. None of his household ever missed unless it was for a birth or death in the family. But, as was fortunate for Victoria, her aunt and cousins all felt the need to take a rest in the afternoon. So she asked her uncle if he could show her around the plantation, knowing full well that he spent Sunday afternoons reading the local newspapers and conferring with the field foreman about the next week's work.

"I'm sorry, Victoria, I really don't have time right now. This is planting season and I really need to confirm which crops go in which fields with Frank. Could you please excuse me?"

"Then can I borrow a buggy and go by myself?" she asked, knowing what the answer would be.

"Now, Victoria, you heard me swear to your Daddy that I'd keep you safe," he started. "I know how independent you can be, but that just isn't proper for a young lady your age."

"How about if someone comes with me, like Sam, maybe?" she asked.

About put up with her insistence, he agreed, with a final, "But be careful!" as she whisked out the door, throwing him a kiss on the way.

"Do you always wrap everybody around your little finger like that?" Sam asked Vicky after they got a distance away from the house.

"Why, Sam, I don't have the faintest idea what you mean," she laughed coyly.

They both sat in silence in the buggy for a while, watching the matched horses pull smoothly and evenly. Then, Victoria broke the silence, "I almost forgot, Sam. I brought you something." She slipped a book from her bag. It was a small copy of Shakespeare's works.

"You didn't need to do that," he replied, somewhat embarrassed at the gift.

"To tell you the truth, my Mom gave it to me. I've read it front to back. It was fine for the classroom, and some parts are good, but it's not my favorite. I wanted you to have it because I didn't know how hard it was to come by books here." She noticed that around Sam she was either very quiet or once she started to talk she couldn't seem to stop.

"I'll be sure to read it front to back, too," he chuckled, "I hear that's the best way to read a book!"

She glanced sideways at him and noticed the laugh lines around his eyes. This put her more at ease and she chuckled also. After that he showed her all around the fields that she remembered from last fall. Then they headed the mares toward the western edge of the plantation, toward where he lived. They had been talking about the party of the night before.

"So, did any young men pursue you last night?" he asked, his voice lower than before.

"I danced almost every dance, but there wasn't any one person special," she commented, without noticing the relief with a sigh that Sam exhaled. "Cousin Sarah was the belle of the ball. She danced with every young man there but, she explained, she had eyes for no one but the young heir of Obici, James."

"Yes," said Sam. "They are a very wealthy family because of their peanut plantation across the river. I hear tell they are thinking of starting their own company to sell their peanuts nationwide. They are very ambitious people."

"Well, if Cousin Sarah were to marry James, she would never have to worry about anything the rest of her life."

With a look of concern in his eyes, Sam turned slightly toward Victoria to see her reaction to his next question, "Does that concern you, Vicky? I mean, having an easy life in high society?"

Stunned, Victoria shot him a look that could have knocked him from the buggy. "You know it doesn't, don't you?" Then she calmed down a little and continued. "I am used to fine things, but my family hasn't always been successful." She told him about the loss of land and income due to the Civil War, about her father moving North because the home plantation wasn't really big enough for both brothers, and about how he had worked hard before the children came along to establish a good business.

"I'm sorry," he said quietly. "I didn't mean to imply that you were only used to a life of ease, I was just..." He couldn't seem to find the right words to continue.

The two of them rode on in silence for a few moments, then Victoria brightened. "Are we getting near where you live?"

"Yes."

"Could I see it, please? And could I meet your family?" she begged. The tone of her voice indicated that she held no resentment at the earlier bit of conversation, so he decided to tell her the truth.

"Vicky, my father is not real fond of Yankees. I've told you our family history before. Are you ready to take the risk? He's not always in a good mood."

"Well, I'm willing to take my chances," she claimed. "Besides, I might not get the chance again for a long time."

Wanting to please her and amazed at her simplistic outlook on life, he decided it might not hurt. So Sam pulled the buggy up in front of a rough hewn log cabin. It had windows on all sides, and appeared very neat from every angle. The calico curtains caught in the breeze and flapped at the open windows, allowing the people inside to foreknow the arrival of guests. A tall, mustached old man came out, followed by a shorter woman who seemed slightly bent, probably with age and child bearing. Three other men came who were unmistakably Sam's brothers, if hair and complexion meant anything. They were James, Walter, and Benjamin, all three being Sam's younger brothers that he had told her about before.

Sam helped Victoria down from the buggy, introduced her, and then offered to go inside to get out of the warm April sun.

It was nearly dinner time when the couple emerged from the cabin again, laughing and cackling about some story just told.

"Now, Miss, you come back and visit us again any time you can," said Javan, Sam's father, with a smile on his face and a twinkle in his eye that showed he had enjoyed a delightful afternoon.

"I'll be sure to do so, thank you," Victoria smiled, as she impulsively took his hand to shake it and then kissed him on the cheek. "Thank you for your hospitality, Mrs. Harrell," she said to Ann, as she shook her hand and then hugged the older woman.

"Good-bye, sugar, you come on back now!" she answered warmly.

Once out of earshot, Sam shook his head, smiling, and said, "Well, you did it again!"

"What's that?" Vicky laughed, good naturedly.

"You could charm the shirt off a man's back, I swear," he laughed in amazement. "I knew my Mom would like you, but I didn't know about my Dad. Now that's probably all I'll hear about from now till kingdom come."

"Is that a bad thing?" she asked with the same coyness she had used earlier.

"No," he chuckled, "It isn't."

Too soon they arrived at the plantation house. As it was starting to get dark, Sam told Victoria to go on in and he would be sure the horses and buggy were put away properly. She was glad to do so to avoid any unnecessary questions from her family, but was sad to leave Sam so abruptly. "Will I see you again?" she whispered.

"I don't know, but now that the ice is broken with my family, please write me. Can I write back to you?"

Risking whatever wrath her mother may have, she said, "Yes, please do. I will welcome each and every one. Good-bye and thank you."

The rest of the week on the plantation seemed uneventful for Victoria. Her aunt made sure to include her in a shopping trip to Suffolk, several teas with community ladies, and even a party and dance held the following Saturday night at a neighbor's house. But she didn't get the opportunity to see Sam again. Either he was in the fields or she was off here or there with her family. So she promised herself that she would pursue this via letter to see where it went. At this point, she told herself, she was just having fun and doing something interesting other than her school work for a change. That was all. Just some harmless fun.

CHAPTER 4

▼

THE RECKONING

Victoria's letters changed over the months. At first she wrote to Sam about all the parties she attended, how her mother kept pushing her to find a suitable beau, and about the drudgery of life in a private school for girls. Later, though, she wondered if he didn't have any knowledge or interest in that sort of thing. So she began to write to him about her family and how she felt about her brothers becoming instrumental in her father's business. She wrote how she felt about being a female at the turn of a new century. She could read, write, speak French, discuss politics, and manage a household, but she couldn't vote. Nothing more than being a wife and mother was expected of her.

His letters never changed. It seemed that he knew from the start what he wanted and how to go about getting it. He wrote her of the beauty of the varying seasons. He wrote her about the miracle of plants growing, rain coming when needed, and a bountiful harvest. He wrote her of his family and the changes that occurred as each grew older. True, he sometimes wrote about her Uncle Arthur and his family and events on the plantation, but it was never a "social" way of doing so. His letters all had an air of sincerity, tenderness, and appreciation for simple things in life that made Victoria long to see the world as he saw it.

Her return trip to Virginia was delayed because of family circumstances in New York. She didn't get to go during fall break because they were embroiled in wedding plans for her older brother Edward. He was to be married at Christmas, and even though his fiancee's family was in charge of most of the planning, her mother insisted that she be allowed to confirm caterers, musicians, places, times, etc. She kept Victoria busy with details that she could have cared less about, yearning to be away from the dirty city and back on the plantation with the earthy sights and smells of harvest time.

Christmas, of course, was a whirlwind of parties and her brother's wedding. She wrote to Sam that it was a gorgeous event and should be for the amount of time and money spent on it. She expressed a desire to live in a simpler mode, and this made him happy to hear her questioning her big city background.

By Spring Break, her sister-in-law was newly pregnant and had the worst morning sickness. The family hired a servant to help around the newlyweds' household, but the poor girl was so unable to help herself, that Victoria was sent to be with her for that week. In her mind, she knew that she was doing something for her family, and she valued that and knew it was a worthy thing to do, but in her heart she longed for the salt air of the Eastern Shore and the plantation. She also wondered, after cleaning up after her sick sister-in-law for the ninth time, if this was worth the trouble.

Meanwhile, the letters kept coming. Usually they came two or three at a time, and she noticed by the dates on them that they were routinely written two days apart.

CHAPTER 5

▼

THE INSIGHT

After the first three months of her sister-in-law's pregnancy were over, life seemed to settle into the same old schedule as before. School, social parties, and sharing news with her Dad about the family business over the dinner table seemed the entirety of Victoria's days. She tired of the routine quickly, and as school was coming to a close, she began to plan her summer vacation.

This year her mother thought staying in New York would be the most exciting thing on earth. With the turn of a new century, people had been giddy about future prospects, and the city had become one giant jubilee. A fourth of July celebration like none ever seen before was planned. There were to be fireworks over the water, a parade, bands playing in all the city's parks, and carnivals set up at easy-to-reach locations around the city. Victoria had to admit that it did sound sort of exciting, but to attend with her mother, father, and older brother was not her idea of a true social event. It was true that several suitors had pursued her during the year, much with the encouragement of her mother. But none seemed to possess the qualities that Victoria found appealing.

Her father had talked to her about business affairs since she was able to understand, so she had a fairly savvy head on her shoulders. Her mother had primed her well on the duties of a lady of high society, so she knew what was expected of her and could easily play the role. But none of the young gentlemen seemed to hold her attention. First had been Robert, who she quickly dismissed the first time they held hands. "Like a wet noodle," she recalled thinking.

Then had come his cousin, Richard. He had wealth beyond compare, but that was all he could talk about. He had no interests other than making more money.

Phillip had been next to pass her mother's inspection, appearing on the scene after a year's stay in Europe. He was well-educated, could speak several languages, knew art, literature, and music, but had no direction in life. He thought he might attend Harvard or Yale or wherever his influential family could place him in the fall. In the meantime, he socialized in the upper crust of New York, living with his family and sponging off them.

One by one each suitor had given up. "What is the matter with you?" her mother sometimes wailed. "Every eligible bachelor in this city has shown interest in you. And you don't even have the decency to give them the time of day!"

"Now, mother, you know that's not true!" she would retort when this ugly conversation started again. "I want to marry for love, not for social standing or money."

Her father would sit nearby, nodding his head slightly, and support her in the argument when necessary, but her mother was exasperated with her one and only daughter becoming what she considered a failure. Her mother felt that the lack of a suitable match for her daughter reflected poorly on her rearing of the child. So when Victoria finally asked to go to Virginia to spend some time during the summer, her mother was more than happy to allow her to go.

"Perhaps you'll have some time to think properly while you're sitting there in the baking sun with no man around who even shows the slightest interest in you," she declared. "You'll come back with a different attitude, young lady, and it will be the best thing for you."

So the time was set that she should take the train south on the first Saturday of June.

As it turned out, Victoria's brother Edward and his wife decided to spend a few days at Cape Charles. His wife was still feeling poorly, although not as sick as during the first three months of her pregnancy. The family felt the fresh air and getting away from the city might do her good. The three of them took the train south, arriving on a pleasant afternoon that was just the right temperature. That evening, to stretch their legs, the three of them walked around the resort town. Their house, one block off Main Street, was of elaborate Victorian styling, just like all of them on that block. Mint green with white trim, it stood out as one of the neatest houses, although each one had distinct trim or colors that set it off from the rest.

"It really is so pretty here," Victoria commented to no one in particular as they strolled along, "I love the quiet, the fresh air, and…oh, listen to the birds."

The three stopped for a moment by someone's wrought iron fence to look high into a maple tree. They spied a family of robins, caring for little ones.

"You would never hear that in New York," her sister-in-law said. "Maybe the birds are there, but no one stops to listen to them."

"Yes," agreed Victoria, "we don't seem to take the time to appreciate simple things, although we spend lots of money on gadgets to help make our lives simpler." She was thinking about the electric lights her Dad had just installed to replace the gas ones at their home here.

A nice looking young man came out the door of the white house they were standing in front of and greeted them warmly. "Enjoying my birds, too?" he asked.

They said yes and then spent a half hour talking to the resident who claimed to live there all year but traveled to the city whenever he needed to on business trips. After the half hour, the three took their leave, having much enjoyed the chat.

"Just think," marveled Victoria, "living here and going to the city only when necessary, just the opposite of us. I think that would be very nice."

"Oh, Victoria," her brother Edward said teasingly, "You have always been the romantic of the family. Longing for simpler things, taking everything at face value, believing everything people say. My goodness, but some days I think Dad had better watch out for you or you'll be heading out toward the great frontier with some swindler or something."

"You never know, Edward," she teased back. "You never know."

Victoria took the ferry across the bay by herself three days later. The fresh air had seemed to do all three of them good. As her brother and sister-in-law parted for the train, she waved good-bye from the ferry, glad to be heading farther south. Her family had not approved of her going by herself, but her Uncle Arthur had assured them that he would be at the landing to pick her up on the other side. She doubted, as she told the others, that she could get into too much trouble on a ferry on the water.

The trip lasted some three hours, and Victoria spent her time reading a book or looking over the railing. She loved the feel of the salt spray on her cheek and wondered what it would be like to be a fisherman and do this every day. "I would probably tire of it after a while," she chuckled to herself dreamily.

As the ferry prepared to dock, she scanned the people on shore, looking for her uncle. Usually he was easy to spot in a crowd with his tall hat that seemed to be a trademark. But she couldn't find it today. She went back to her seat, put her book in her bag, and gathered up her other belongings. It really was too much for her to carry alone, but she expected help at any moment.

The boat landed and the gangplank was set down. The other passengers filed off one at a time, some greeting others like they had been apart for a long while, and others going about their business in the usual manner. Still she didn't see her uncle. She paused, perplexed, when suddenly out of the crowd came a shocking red head that purposefully pushed its way through the crowd and up the plank.

"There you are!" he cried. "Sorry I'm late. I hope you weren't too worried."

Victoria, almost beside herself with joy and surprise, couldn't speak for a moment. She felt like she wanted to rush into this man's arms and hug him as an old friend or savior, but she restrained from it. Instead, she stretched out her gloved hand, shook his, and said, "Thank you for coming to get me. Is everything alright with Uncle Arthur and his family?"

"Yes," he explained quickly, "Your cousin Elizabeth chose today to go into labor. They are all a little preoccupied with delivering a baby. So your uncle asked if I could come get you, which I was pleased to be able to do." He grinned sideways at her, a little awkwardly.

"My goodness," Victoria replied, "I thought she wasn't due for another week or so."

"It's not uncommon for a child to come into this world when it feels it's ready to do so," Sam commented, as if he were an expert on the matter. Victoria thought his simple knowledge of "life" a little odd for a man, but she then remembered how many infants in his family had died at birth and thought to herself that maybe he knew more about it than he let on.

"Well, then," she said as she began to gather her bags, "Let's get going! I don't want to miss something as exciting as this!"

Sam helped her with her baggage and made sure she was situated comfortably in the carriage before they hurried off toward Sunbury. As it turned out, they needn't have hurried, for Elizabeth was still laboring when they arrived. She had been moved early in the labor from her own house two miles down the road to home, so that there would be plenty of help around after the baby arrived. So all the action was taking place in her old room upstairs when they arrived. After they had deposited Victoria's baggage in the guest bedroom and said a quick hello to her uncle and cousins, there was little for them to do but wait, so the couple went out under a great magnolia tree in the front yard and sat.

"How long do these things take?" Victoria asked, more rhetorically than anything.

"Oh, I've known this to go on for a full day," Sam replied, "but that wasn't good on either the baby or the mother." The sudden misting in his eyes and the tone of concern in his voice made Victoria realize that he truly was more knowledgeable than she on the matter of child bearing. She wondered how much he had seen and how deeply his heart had been broken by just such an unfortunate delivery. She hesitated, uncertain as of how to begin, then she took his hand, squeezed it, and asked, "Would you like to tell me about it?"

He took a deep breath then began, "My family hasn't always been able to afford for a doctor to come in at a birthing," he began. "To us, birthing is just a natural part of life. But looking back on it, I wonder if we would have had a doctor on hand, maybe those little ones would still be alive." He just shook his head as the sadness seemed to overwhelm him. He paused for a moment, then continued. "I was there for the birthing of Richard's babies and Rosa's. When we knew it was going to happen, the family went to their houses. Mama set up shop, so to speak, keeping us all busy with boiling water, preparing clean cloths for the baby, cleaning out sponges, and so on. There's even more work after the baby comes, with cleaning up the afterbirth and getting the mother cleaned up. Of course, Mama didn't let us boys right in the room with her, but sometimes we peeked in and we could always hear the crying out and moaning."

He paused again, seeming to be relieved to share these unpleasant memories with someone. Then he went on, "Richard's wife's first delivery had been fairly easy. It took only about eight hours. I remember because we got there right around dark and the baby was born right around daybreak. Mama says the first one is the hardest. So we didn't expect any trouble with the second one. But she was breech. That means she was coming feet first instead of head first," he added, not knowing if she was familiar with the terminology or not. "She tore at Susan, Richard's wife, right well. We had a time getting that mess cleaned up afterward. But the poor little thing. It exhausted her so, that she had no breath once she finally got into this world. Died right then and there on the spot. There was blood, Vicky, lots and lots of blood."

Sam took a deep breath and then went on. "With Rosa's baby it was different. The delivery all seemed to be normal, but when the little girl was born, she wasn't shaped quite right in the head. She seemed to be, well, missing something. She wasn't nice and round like a normal baby, or even the pointed head of some that have a tough time coming into this world. She was flat on top. Well, she lived only a couple of hours. It about tore Rosa up, to have to look at her child so deformed and have to nurse her and hold her. She was hurting, physically and emotionally. And I remember her just crying and crying. We all did. And then the little thing just shuddered and stopped breathing. That was it.

Again he paused, but only for a brief moment. It seemed to Victoria that once this gate had been opened, the flood of emotions behind it had to flow out, so he kept going, "Now don't get me wrong, bringing a baby into this world is a beautiful thing. A miraculous thing. I've gotten to hold other babies that were just fine. And God bless them. They are the softest, most delicate little creatures. When they reach out and grab your finger or touch your face, well, your heart just melts. And all you want to do is just hold them close to yourself and protect them for all you're worth. But these little ones that die without a chance, well, God bless them even more."

He finally stopped, looked up in surprise that he had gone on for so long, and noticed that his hand still held hers. In a moment of self-awareness, he wiped a tear from his cheek with his other hand and squeezed her hand with the one still holding it. "I hope I don't seem weak to you. That was probably more than you bargained for," he sighed.

"No, Sam, thank you for sharing that with me," she said quietly, as she kept her hand in his. "Please, let's not ever have any secrets or hurts between you and me. Let's share those things. It's a lot easier burden when two carry it rather than one."

Wondering about the full meaning of what she had just said, he nodded in agreement,

"Yes, life would be better that way. I hope I haven't filled you with fear for your cousin."

"No, actually. She's young; she's healthy. I see no reason to fear."

She fanned herself with her hat, noticing that the day seemed unseasonably warm and that it must be getting around 4:00 in the afternoon. The two sat in silence for a while. Victoria wondered at how her sister-in-law would get along with birthing. She had been so sick and seemed so frail compared to Elizabeth. All she could do was hope and pray for the best.

Finally, the great doors to the brick plantation house opened and her uncle came striding out with a look of pure ecstasy on his face. "There you are, niece! Sorry we didn't have time to greet you properly before. Been a little busy around here, you know." He grinned like a man who had some great secret.

Victoria and Sam had dropped hands and now got up as she raced to the house and into her uncle's arms. "Oh, please, uncle, tell us how they're doing!" she cried.

"I have a grandson!" her uncle shouted, unable to contain himself any longer. He swung Victoria around on the broad porch and danced a little jig like a man half his age. "Finally! A boy in the house!" Then he chuckled and plucked Victoria under the chin, "Not that I've ever minded having a brood of girls, you know. God knows I've loved each and every one of you. But finally, enough of lace and ruffles and coming out parties. Now I can look forward to roller skates and bicycles and pony rides and worms and, oh my goodness." He seemed so overwhelmed and his smile just seemed to go on across his face until it would crack in two. He plopped himself down on the rail.

"And Cousin Elizabeth? How is she?" Victoria asked, almost not wanting to spoil this precious, happy moment.

"Oh, she's fine too. Sturdy as an ox, that one. Good solid girls I raised, yes, sir. Good solid Virginia girls, Sam, nothing better."

Sam had come up onto the porch and witnessed the whole scene. Now he seemed surprised but pleased to be included in the glad tidings. He fervently shook his benefactor's hand with a warm, "Congratulations, sir. Many good wishes for both the mother and the wee one."

"Yes, Sam, yes indeed. Well said." Uncle Arthur just sat there beaming, looking off toward the west. Then, as if remembering something, he said, "Oh, excuse my manners, Sam, I haven't thanked you for fetching Victoria for us. What with all the excitement, I clean forgot that you had to take a day off work on our behalf. Thank you, son."

Now it was Sam's turn to beam. The term of affection had not gone unnoticed on his part. Again he shook Uncle Arthur's hand and said, "Sir, it was my pleasure. You know I would do anything to help the family out. Anything. Anytime."

Victoria wondered if the warmth that passed between them was a product of the happy occasion or was an outward expression of inner feelings. Either way, she relished in seeing her uncle and Sam so affectionate toward each other.

The three stood there for a moment, basking in the sun. Then Sam said those inevitable words she was dreading to hear, "Well, sir, I guess I had better go share the good news with my family and get some chores done before sunset. Is there anything else you need me for?"

"No, no. You're quite right. The livestock must be fed no matter what our lives consist of, so off you go and please share the glad tidings with your family. Thanks again."

Sam headed off the porch and waved as he strode across the broad grassy area in front of the house, heading toward the barn.

"There goes a good man, Victoria," her uncle said after him. "I have grown to love him like a son. He's a hard worker, has a level head on his shoulders, and seems to want to move up in this world, but not at the expense of any other living soul. A lady could do a lot worse than him."

"Yes, uncle, I agree." Victoria answered, trying to keep her heart from pounding so loudly that her uncle could hear it. "I agree."

They were quiet for a few moments, each lost in their own happy thoughts and warm feelings. Standing against the porch railing, side by side, some kindred spirit united the old man and his niece. He stretched his arm around her waist and drew her close. "It is good to have you here again. Now," and with this he let her go and jumped around again as they heard a baby cry from inside, "let's go see that grandson of mine."

The next few weeks were some of the happiest of Victoria's life. Everyone around Sunbury was exceedingly happy. The family doted on the new baby, named Arthur Milton, after each of his grandfathers, but for convenience had decided to call him Art. In fact, the family spent so much time waiting on Elizabeth and the baby, that Victoria had plenty of time to spend outside and with Sam. One thing that she noticed was that Art liked to have a feeding right around sunrise. Victoria could hear his gentle cries from Elizabeth's room next to hers, and once the sun was up she found it impossible to go back to sleep again. So she took to quietly getting up and going outside to enjoy the cool air. It seemed to her that the late afternoons were hotter than usual, so she enjoyed sitting quietly under the magnolia where she and Sam had awaited the birth and shared memories. As she sat there on a bench, she would listen to the birds singing a chorus of welcome for the new day. Truly, she thought, this is as close to heaven as there is on earth. The freshness of a new day, the birds, the cool breeze off the water gently brushed her cheek. There couldn't be another place so perfect.

Sometimes she would see Sam cutting across the yard on his way to the barn to do the morning chores. It became his habit to come rest with her for a few minutes after giving the animals their feed and turning them out to pasture. He could only spare a few moments before he headed for the fields, but those moments were as precious to her as any they had ever spent together. Now, in this special spot, they held hands. She was cautious at first, keeping their hands hidden under a fold of her dress. But as the days wore on and no one admonished them for this early morning rendezvous, they became a little bolder and held hands openly.

"Oh, Sam," she started out of a peaceful reverie, "It is so wonderful here. I love hearing the morning birds."

"Then I shall give you a pet name. One that only I use for you. I shall call you 'Birdie.'"

Victoria looked at him astonished. "What? Oh, please, no, Sam. I know a Birdie in New York. She is the most awful old crow you could ever find. She is loud and always cawing here and there. Her real name is Roberta, of course, but I could never be fond of a nickname like that, no matter how well intentioned you meant it," she said in a disgusted tone.

"That's fine. I will take the first letter of your name and put the two together. How about Virdie, then?" he soothed.

"Virdie? I never heard of such!" she chuckled. Then seeing the seriousness in his eyes about having a pet name for her, she relented. "Alright, Virdie it is. But just between you and me."

Several days later they were again under the old magnolia tree. They found themselves holding hands again, as naturally as if they had always done it.

"Sam?" she asked, "I know my uncle is fond of you. Do you think he would approve of us?"

Sam paused for a moment before he spoke, like he often did, "I don't know, Vicky, but I know that I do. And if you do, then I think that's all that really matters."

She had to think about what he had just said, then intuitively sensing that she perhaps had more to give up in this matter than he did, she hesitated, knit her brow deep in thought, then responded, "Yes, you are right. That is all that matters."

The fourth of July celebration for the year 1900 was the most spectacular that anyone had ever seen. Many cities sponsored parades, fireworks, and dances. Uncle Arthur's family attended, enjoying the rare treat of a day out in the middle of the week. Even some of the family servants and hired hands went with them, including Sam and his brothers Walt and Ben. James had been feeling poorly again, partly due to the heat, so he and their parents had stayed at home. Even though they spent the day together, Sam and Victoria didn't have an opportunity to be alone. They were both saddened, knowing that her time in Virginia would soon be at an end.

"Do you really have to go back to New York?" Sam asked her when they finally had a moment alone together.

"Yes, I've been here a month and I don't want to wear out my welcome! Besides, Susan will be delivering her baby soon and I'm sure I will be needed to help around there."

"Virdie?" he practically whispered to her, "I don't want to lose you. I'm concerned that you'll go back to New York and your Mom will talk you into marrying some fancy rich city man. I'm not asking you to not go to parties and such, but I just want you to know that you've captured my heart and I freely give it to you."

Saying that, he slipped something into her hand. She squeezed his hand quickly and then opened hers. It was a tiny heart locket. "Oh, Sam!" she exclaimed. "This is beautiful! You didn't have to...I mean, it's really not...oh, I mean..." Realizing that she sounded like she was rejecting him, she quickly pulled herself together and said, "Sam, I love you, too, but I have to go. I promise I will be back and then you and I can spend more time together. In the meantime, I consider us engaged and we'll write each other. Often, alright?"

"Oh, yes, thank you." he said in relief.

"No, Sam, thank you."

CHAPTER 6

▼

THE WAITING

The crops that fall were some of the best ever seen in that area. The ears of corn were large and full. The tobacco and peanuts were plentiful. The soybeans and wheat exceeded any harvest known yet. Even the fishing industry seemed to be picking up. Everything was good. The warm weather held out into December, long after all the crops were in. Sam and his family had made more money off their portion of the ten acres that Victoria's Uncle Arthur leased to them than they had imagined possible. The family considered what to do next. Several options presented themselves immediately: to try to buy a small farm of their own or to stay where they were was a matter of great discussion. Ultimately, it was Walter who made the final decision.

It was in December. Walt and Ben had gone into the woods hunting to get a wild turkey for the family's Christmas dinner. They had walked around for an hour or so when they flushed one out of a small thicket on the edge of a field. As Walt aimed his gun and pulled the trigger, the old muzzle loader back fired. Perhaps it was dirty, perhaps it was jammed due to humidity, or perhaps it was just a freak accident. But as it was, Walt would have died there on the spot bleeding to death had Ben not been with him.

Ben quickly tried to stop the bleeding and noticed that a good portion of Walt's right arm was just dangling by the bone. Besides that, Walt had covered his right eye with his hand and refused to put it down. "I think I'm blind!" he screamed.

Ben wrapped the arm, using his coat as a make shift sling and then packing moss in the wound to stop the blood. It was so close to Walt's shoulder that he couldn't make anything as a tourniquet. Then they headed to the closest farm, which happened to be Sunbury. Ben's mind raced as he tried to figure out what to do first to help Walt the most. He walked with him across the field, then propped him up against a fence rail and ran to get help. The moss had not stopped the blood much at all, and he knew he had to get help fast. So he ran and as soon as he felt he could be heard, he started yelling.

Uncle Arthur immediately came out of the house to see what the commotion was about. Ben gave him a quick synopsis of the accident then, thankfully, Uncle Arthur took control.

"I'm going to tell Frank to go fetch the doctor. You go to the barn and hitch up the old mare and the wagon. Put some clean blankets in the back and a bale of hay. I'll meet you back out here as quickly as possible. Now, go!"

Ben took off running again and hitched up the wagon as quickly as he could. He thanked God now that he had spent time learning how to do it correctly the first time from his older brother Sam. In just a few minutes he met Uncle Arthur in front of the house. He, in the meantime, had sent Frank for the doctor, the women to fix up a bed in the parlor on the first floor, a servant to get Walt and Ben's family, and had picked up his own personal first aid kit that he kept in the pantry. Then the two of them raced down the road to where Walt lay, semi-conscious.

"Walt, we're back. I got help. Hang in there." Ben pleaded as the two men tried to gently but quickly lift his frame onto the wagon without disturbing the arm too much. Then they raced back to the house. They had just settled him into the portable bed when the doctor arrived.

"He's pretty bad off," Uncle Arthur whispered when the doctor walked in with a raised eyebrow. Taking one look, he nodded, commanded everyone out of the room except Frank, and shut the door.

As they stepped into the hallway, Ben asked Uncle Arthur, "Will he be alright?"

"I don't know, son," Uncle Arthur said as he put his arm around Ben's shoulders. "But we can hope and pray for the best."

Within ten minutes, the rest of the family arrived and the story of what happened had to be told all over again. It made Ben sick to the stomach to even think about it, and everyone could tell he felt awful, responsible in some way.

"Now, Ben," his mother crooned, "It was just an accident. You didn't cause it and you did everything you could to help him. You may have even saved his life. So you don't go putting no blame on yourself for all this."

Ben just bit his lip, looked at his feet, and said nothing, trying to hold back the tears. After a while, he thought to ask Uncle Arthur why he had been dismissed from the room, too.

"Oh, that's simple," answered Uncle Arthur with almost a chuckle. "After four babies and who knows how many farm accidents, Doc knows I'm the biggest baby that ever was. I pass out at the slightest sight of blood and he'd end up having to doctor me, too."

The family smiled some, then Ben said, "But you didn't! You helped me load him into the wagon and bring him in here. You did fine."

"True. When I have to, I can be strong, but even just thinking about it gives me weak knees."

The rest of the family attempted small talk for a while to take their minds off their horrible thoughts of what was happening to Walt, but even that dwindled. Each sat in the hallway, lost in their own emotions.

After what seemed like an eternity, the doctor stepped out of the room and quietly closed the door behind him. Everyone, including Uncle Arthur's family, jumped to their feet, but he motioned them to sit and be still.

"Walter is a very lucky man," he began. "He has lost a lot of blood, his arm, and his eye. But thanks to his brother's quick thinking, he still has his life."

Everyone caught their breath in this grim prognosis.

The doctor continued, "It will take quite a while for him to recover from the loss of blood. I was able to sew the arm back on, but the muscles are severed to the point that I could not restore them. He will never regain use of the arm. It will simply dangle there uselessly. But at least he has one. As for his eye, it was impossible to save. The black powder had burnt it beyond repair. So I did what I could, which wasn't much. He will need to wear an eye patch after this. He will never regain sight in that eye. I'm sorry, but I did the best I could."

The family didn't move for a few moments, seeming to have to think about everything that was just said to comprehend the full intent of it all. Then, slowly, as they came to grips with it, they began to thank the doctor for what he had done.

Finally, the doctor said, "I recommend that you not move him for at least two weeks. He needs to rest and regain his strength. After that, we can move him home, but he will still need more time to recuperate. After a month or so, then we can talk about some rehabilitation. He will need to learn how to do things with only one arm and one eye. There will be a lot of things he won't be able to do. But let's talk about that later. For now, I'm sure you want to see him. He's asleep and he needs his rest, so don't wake him."

Victoria's mother had realized for a while that her daughter was receiving letters from someone in Virginia. As a polite, Victorian, well-bred lady she assumed they were from a suitor whom her daughter had met at one of her Uncle Arthur's parties, so she asked no questions. But the thought that her daughter couldn't find a suitable mate in the great expanse of eligible bachelors of New York City troubled her. What was this young fellow's family like? Were they one of the "first families of Virginia?" But she kept quiet, hoping that Victoria would come to her and confide in her. Until the day before Christmas.

The mail had arrived late that day, supposedly due to the heavier amount than usual. When Victoria received her letter, she ran to her room, as she usually did. But very soon her mother heard a cry of dismay and then weeping. Feeling that she could wait no longer and fearing that her daughter had been dismissed from the young man's affections, and on the day before Christmas, how uncouth!, she knocked on Victoria's bedroom door and then entered before the door was opened for her.

"Victoria, dear, what is this all about?"

Her daughter was so distraught that they only thing she could do was hold out the letter. Her mother noticed immediately that the hand-writing was not flowery or smooth like so many Victorian ladies of the time. Yes, it was definitely masculine penmanship. The paper was rough, not like the embossed stationary that she used. As she read the contents, the heading jumped out at her. "My dearest Virdie,"

"Who is Virdie?" she asked without thinking.

"I am, of course, mother," she replied, "It's a nick name just between Sam and myself."

Her mother read further. It seemed to be the common Christmas greetings and wishes for the best. Then she came to the part about Walt's accident. It seemed that not many gory details had been spared.

"And who is Walt?"

"That is one of Sam's younger brothers," Victoria replied with a tone to her voice that indicated affection and yet impatience that her mother didn't know the fact.

"Alright, dear," her mother said as she looked up from the letter and settled herself onto the bed beside her daughter. Having never been very close, she felt a bit uncomfortable at this, but knew it was time for a talk that she had been hoping to avoid. "Tell me all about it."

"Couldn't we wait until Daddy was here?" Victoria tried to stall.

"No. You know he stays late with his employees on Christmas eve and once he gets home we'll be decorating the tree and people will be stopping by for egg nog and the house will be busy. Besides, I think this is girl talk. So, let's have it."

Over the next hour the two women talked and cried and talked some more. Victoria's mother was amazed at how mature her daughter's perception of the world had become in the last year or so. She talked about child bearing and birth and death in a way that she never had, with a candidness that caused her Victorian up-bringing to blush.

On the other hand, she was dismayed to discover that Sam was a common farm hand. Hearing the affection and admiration in her daughter's voice caused more than one moment when she had to fight to keep control of her emotions and not explode in platitudes about their own social standing and all she herself had hoped for her own daughter. All that she had worked so hard for. Social standing, servants, and a life of ease seemed to lack priority to her daughter. Couldn't she see how much she would miss all these things? Couldn't she see that she could never fit into a lower class society? Apparently not, her mother concluded, trying to control her temper.

In the course of the hour they argued a little, but her mother fully believed this was a temporary fling. If she kept her daughter away from this man long enough, she would forget about him. When her father came home, she would take up the matter with him. Then he could talk some sense into this child that seemed to favor him above all else. "If anyone can talk some sense into her, he can." she told herself as she left Victoria's room with an uneasy feeling.

It wasn't until late that night when all the social obligations were finished that they had a quiet moment to themselves. "William?" she began hesitantly, "let's take an egg nog into the parlor. Just you and me. And talk."

Victoria's father was so taken aback by this unusual request that he complied with no questions asked. Once they were settled in front of the fire, her mother began her story. Her opening line was, "I have something to tell you about Victoria. Please control yourself until I am finished because I need you to straighten this thing out for me. She won't listen to me, but she'll listen to you."

After a half hour of emotional tirade and a lot of finger pointing at him for allowing his daughter to "traipse all over kingdom come unattended," she finished with "Now go talk some sense into her."

"Inez," he began calmly, "I know what you have always desired for Victoria. But that's your life, not hers. That's your dream, not hers. She has got to be allowed to make decisions such as this on her own. We have raised her to be level-headed, thoughtful of others, kind, and sincere. At the moment you see those qualities as undesirable because the object of her affection is not one of your choosing. Inez, she's almost 19 years old. She's at the age to fall in love and marry. And I, for one, encourage her to marry for love instead of social standing. Sometimes I tire of all the charades that you put on. I sometimes think that you care more about what the tabloids think of you than I do. Now I will go talk to her, but I doubt that it will be in the way you hoped."

At that, he got up, excused himself, and went up the long winding stairs to his daughter's room. He quietly knocked on the door, knowing that she wouldn't be asleep with all of the day's emotions swimming through her head. He was right.

"Come in," she called. "Oh, Daddy! I'm so glad you came up. I'm sorry that Mother has given you an earful tonight, on Christmas Eve." Then she broke into tears.

"Come here, pumpkin," he said as he sat on the edge of her bed and gathered her in his arms like he did when she was little. "This is so much my fault, I fear. I have treated you equally as your brothers. I know your mother fears I have given you too many freedoms and now you will use those to turn against her and every-thing she holds dear. But, truly," and with this he held her face in his hand, wiped her tears with the other and had her look into his eyes, "do you love him?"

"Yes, Daddy," she said without a moment's hesitation and without averting her gaze. "I do. When I am with him, I feel whole. I feel protected. I feel warm and safe. There has only been one other time when I ever felt that way."

"When was that, darling?" William asked, fearing some other revelation of a clandestine love affair.

"Whenever I'm with you, Daddy," she responded, laying her head against his shoulder and melting his heart as only she could do and had done for years.

With that, he resolved to help her all he could, even against her Mother's wishes, but knew that he would have to be careful to not upset a careful balance in their household.

"Victoria, it's Christmas. The house will be brimming with people again tomorrow as your brother and his family come to visit and others, too. Your Mother will undoubtedly act as if nothing has happened. I know you. I know you would love to jump on the first train south and be there for them. And I know they need you. You have a good heart, child, but pour it out into a letter. Write a long one right now and I will make sure it is posted day after tomorrow first thing. In the meantime, I suspect your Mother won't allow any trips on your own. So it's easier to go along with that than upset her. Then we'll see what we can work out later. Agreed?"

Victoria, who had always worshiped her father, readily agreed. As a child, she had thought he was a god, but now, as a maturing woman, she appreciated how sensible he was and how well he handled people. "No wonder he's a successful business man," she thought to herself.

"Yes, Daddy, thank you." she sniffled one last time as he got up, gave her a hug, and left. She crossed the room to her cherry, Queen Anne's writing desk and pulled out ink and pen. Then she sat down to write to Sam the longest letter yet.

Christmas Day itself came and went in a whirlwind of friends and family dropping in and out of the house. Most of the family doted on Edward and Susan's baby daughter, Evelyn, who was now one month old. Victoria held her for a while, but didn't see anything particularly interesting in this little creature. She let her mother and father do most of the cooing and babbling and found a good reason to excuse herself fairly early in the day so that she could retreat into her own thoughts about babies, men, and what the coming year might bring for her.

Victoria's nineteenth birthday came and went without much fanfare. In her mother's eyes, she was sulking, but at least she hadn't asked to make any travel plans. Victoria, on the other hand, spent her days pouring over books and throwing herself into her lessons with a renewed fervor. She instinctively felt that this might be her last chance at such an opportunity, and she and Sam knew it would be sinful to waste it. Every evening she sat and wrote to him. She explained her longing to be with him and her desire to spend time with him, but lamented the restrictions put on her by her mother. As Spring break approached, she felt a renewed hope that a trip might be possible, but her mother filled her days with charity work and visiting her side of the family around the city. Edward, Susan, and baby Evelyn came to spend Easter with them. Much of that day was spent in playing with the good natured baby, but there was still a void in Victoria's heart that couldn't be filled.

In May, her mother commented one day that she was proud of the way Victoria had excelled in her studies the last few months. So much so, she said, that she was planning something special after final exams were completed. Victoria could only hope it meant traveling southward.

Of course, it didn't, at first. But finally her father's good sense won out. It had been several years since her mother had been to the house at Cape Charles. Victoria, knowing that it was rare for her father to be terribly assertive with her mother, imagined the conversation something like this:

"Inez, we haven't been to the Cape Charles house for a while. Let's plan to go for a week or so in June after Victoria is done with her lessons."

"William, you are just trying to help that girl in her wayward path. No, Sir. I will not go anywhere with her unless it is north or far away from that rough-handed, ill-bred, child stealer."

Now, Inez, you know nothing of his character. Surely you think Victoria has better judgment than to fall in love with a child stealer."

"You always side with her. You always have. And always against me," here her mother's voice raised. That happened when she got excited and forgot about good grammar of complete sentences.

Her father would almost chuckle, but would calmly remove his glasses, take her mother's hand, and reply, "Inez, think. The longer we try to keep her away from this man, the more her heart yearns for him. Let's go there and meet him for ourselves. Let's be supportive of her. Let's allow her to make some decisions on her own. We've brought her up right. She'll make good decisions. I fear that if we don't, we'll lose her completely. Would you rather have that?"

Realizing that her husband was right, common sense won Inez over. It was true. Victoria was now 19 years old. If she wanted to run off and marry some street urchin, she could. She had money of her own and knew how to use it. So, resigned to the fact that what must be, must be, her mother capitulated, but her heart ached.

Once settled in the Cape Charles house, William sent word across the bay to his brother Arthur to come visit. He invited his whole family and included a special note that he wished to meet Sam. Arthur, upon receiving this letter from his brother and realizing that even Victoria and Inez were along, was surprised. He wondered what was going on that they all had been invited to come over and spend a few days. It was true that he welcomed the time away from his office. He hadn't taken any kind of trip for years, but he had been busy, he reasoned, with his insurance business and his plantation. But the planting was done, and the other farm business could be handled by Frank, as most of it was already done by him anyhow. So he closed up shop, went home and told Verna, Sarah, Mary, and Margaret to pack their things for a few days on the beach. Then he went to look for Sam, whom he found in the barn, just as he assumed he would.

"Sam?" he began, as the younger man looked up from currying a mare, "We've been invited to my brother's beach house in Cape Charles."

"Congratulations, sir," Sam replied, knowing how hard the old man worked and sincerely glad that he should be able to relax for a few days. "When do you and the girls leave?"

"No, Sam, I don't think you understand. 'We' includes you."

"Me, Sir?" Sam was incredulous. "Why me?"

Arthur explained as best he could figure. As a look of understanding dawned in Sam's eyes, Arthur asked him openly, "I'm as puzzled by it as you. But, Sam, will you fill me in now on what you think of this?"

So Sam put down the curry brush, closed the gate to the horse's stall, and proceeded to tell Arthur how fond he and Victoria had become of each other. He ended up telling the old gentleman his dreams of owning his own farm some day and making a good living for the two of them. He sensibly commented that he knew she was giving up a lot to be with him and expressed his strong desire to be worthy of her affection and love.

With his heart poured out, he looked into Arthur's eyes and blushed, "I'm sorry, sir. I know I have over-stepped the bounds of a hired hand, but I, I mean we, never meant to fall in love. It just happened."

"Sam, my boy," Arthur said, slapping him on the back, "I wouldn't have it any other way. You are a fine, hard-working young man. You are kind to animals, children, and women alike. You are fair in your dealing with men. You have worthwhile dreams. I support you. I would much rather one of my daughters marry for love than for social standing. Yes, it would be nice to have a fine house and servants and no worries of food and clothes, but without love, well, it's just a big house and food and clothes. Love means happiness, Sam. I have been truly blessed by the good Lord above. I have it all. I have love; I have material possessions; I have people I respect. And you're one of them, Sam. I know I can always count on you around here. You're reliable. I wish it were one of my girls who had fallen in love with you. The only thing the good Lord didn't see fit to bless me with was a son. But, Sam, I feel that fondness toward you. So, you have my blessing to marry Victoria. I will do everything in my power to help you do so."

Arthur, who had always been open and affectionate with people, was not surprised at himself. Sam, however, seemed quite uneasy at the extent of feelings shown toward him. All he could say was, "Thank you, Sir, I hope I always merit this trust."

Arthur, then, who also had a practical side to him, said, "Alright, then, I will call in the tailor tomorrow. He will have to make a new suit for you post haste.

Oh, it can be done alright, just a little tricky. He makes those dresses up for the womenfolk quick enough; it's about time he makes a man's suit just as well."

"Sir?" questioned Sam. "I don't have the money for a fancy new suit right now."

"I didn't say you needed any money, did I? This one's on me. If you're going to marry my niece, then you'd better dress the part. Her father will feel toward you the way I do. He's a man like me; he can appreciate hard work and an honest heart. Her mother, on the other hand, will not be so easily won over. But, mind your p's and q's and you'll be fine. In time, she'll be alright. You mark my words, just wait and see."

Thus it was that Sam was fitted the next morning for a suit and was packed and ready to go by the following morning. He could not have been more nervous as he and Arthur's family stepped onto the Virginia Ferry Company's newest boat to take them across the bay to Cape Charles.

Sam paced the deck of the ferry boat as it steamed across the water. Uncle Arthur's family sat quietly, barely looking out across the bay.

"Sam, for heaven's sake, sit down," Verna said. "You're wearing out your new shoes!"

Sam stopped, looked down, and then said, "Yes, ma'am." and obediently sat down.

They had no fear or trepidation as he did about this trip. A hundred different questions ran through his head at once, falling and stumbling over each other till he felt he was in such a state that he may never think straight again. "Sir?" he began, directed at Arthur, "Thank you again for all you've done for me."

"Sam, you're welcome again. Now, relax. You'll be fine. There isn't anything to not like about you. Inez may be a tough nut to crack, but if anyone can do it, you can." Then he smiled his biggest smile at Sam and patted him on the shoulder.

The younger man tried to relax.

Very soon the ferry was pulling alongside Cushman's dock. There on the edge was Victoria, sandwiched between her father and mother. Sam looked them over from afar, trying not to appear obvious. Her mother, Inez Brittanhaur, seemed impeccably dressed, her back straight and hair fashionably done. Her father, William Brittanhaur, looked more at ease. He waved and smiled and seemed to enjoy every moment of life with a twinkle in his eye.

Uncle Arthur's family was all lined up along the railing now and they waved back, everyone calling out hello's. Sam stood there beside his mentor and protector, almost paralyzed by fear.

"Wave, son, and you'll be fine," Arthur whispered as he nudged him in the ribs.

Sam obeyed and then they lurched forward awkwardly as the boat came to a halt. Sam and Arthur turned and picked up the ladies' suitcases and hat boxes. It seemed they had packed everything they owned for their three days' stay. Arthur repeated to Sam as they leaned over to pick up luggage, "You'll be fine. I guarantee it. Trust me. Now smile and follow me."

Sam did so, glad of the guidance and glad to have Arthur's large form ahead of him on which to focus. They went down the gang plank to where the womenfolk were all hugging each other's necks. Arthur went to his brother first, shook his hand fervently and with great affection. Then he bowed to Inez then hugged her, then he hugged Victoria and kissed her on the cheek.

"Obviously this was a family that showed a great deal of affection to each other," Sam thought, "not like mine." Then it was his turn.

"William," started Arthur, "let me introduce you to my most valuable employee, Samuel Harrell."

Sam quickly set down the suitcases in his right hand and stretched it forth.

William reached forward and grabbed Sam's hand warmly, and each man noticed the firmness and strength of the other. Sizing each other up quickly, each mutely decided that they liked the other immediately.

"Now, Sam, over here please," Arthur continued. "This is my most wonderful sister-in-law..." at which point he was interrupted.

"Arthur Brittanhaur, I am your only sister-in-law!" At that they all chuckled and the tension was greatly relieved.

"As I was saying, Inez, may I introduce you to Samuel Harrell?"

"My pleasure, ma'am," Sam got out as he bowed courteously to her. She stretched forth her hand, and not knowing what else to do with it, Sam kissed the top of it gently.

"Oh, my," Inez started, surprised, "How do you do?"

"Fine, thank you, ma'am," he answered. It was then that their eyes met. He could see that she had a harder shell than the rest of the family, but that there was a warmth there, a flicker of an ember that he determined to fan into a flame of affection before the three days were ended.

She, for her part, looked into his amazingly blue eyes and saw a maturity beyond his years. She felt the roughness of his hand even through her glove. She wasn't sure if that pleased her or not, but she made a mental note of it.

William had continued in a natural tone, "And of course you remember Victoria."

"Yes, of course, good day to you," Sam stuttered out, finally fully facing her and feeling his red complexion turning redder even though he wished it were not so.

Victoria greeted him as warmly as she felt she dared under the circumstances, "Good morning, Sam. It is good to see you again."

After that the party of nine paraded to William's house on Second Street, where the luggage was taken up to the bedrooms. Fortunately, the house was sufficiently large to accommodate them all, even if privacy was somewhat lacking. Sarah and Victoria would share a room. Mary and Margaret shared a room. Of course, the elder Brittanhaur brothers shared rooms with their wives, and Sam was fortunate enough to have a room to himself. It was the smallest of the upstairs rooms, but he was grateful for being treated like family. He had been concerned that he might be expected to sleep in a servant's quarters or a guest house in the backyard. When asked if his room was acceptable to him, he quickly told his host, "More than I ever hoped for, sir."

William could tell from his honest, quick answers that Sam was an intelligent man. His brother had told him of Sam's abilities with machines and his quickness to learn new things, so he was quite pleased to meet this object of his daughter's affections and found no flaw in him save the flaming red hair.

As soon as was feasible, William got Arthur aside. A loose shingle on the out house seemed sufficient excuse for the two of them to slip away from the chattering ladies, who probably wouldn't have noticed their absence anyway.

"O.K. Arthur, tell me about Samuel, and don't leave anything out on my account."

Arthur smiled and began, remembering the sincere concern that a father has for a daughter who is of marriageable age. "He's quick to learn. He attends church regularly. He is invaluable to me around the plantation. He's…"

"Yes, yes, yes." William interrupted. "I know all that. Now tell me what I really want to know."

As only two brothers could who knew each other's feelings well, they spent the next hour in the back yard. Arthur filled William in on the sadness and misfortune that seemed to surround the Harrell family. He ended with, "But this boy seems to rise above that. Truly, William, if Victoria were my daughter, I would be proud to have Sam as a son-in-law. I wouldn't ever worry if she were being treated right. They may have hard times together, but they will know love and happiness."

"Thank you, Arthur," William said. "You have answered a myriad of questions for me with the good judgment and common sense that I felt too emotionally unstable in this situation to provide for myself. You have lifted a great weight from my mind. Thank you, dear brother." At this the younger brother shook the older brother's hand fervently and thankfully.

The older brother, always with the role of protector, advisor, and friend in mind, replied, "William, that was easy. You and I both know that the hard part is going to be convincing your dear wife of anything."

"Yes, I agree," William sighed, "but I think we don't need to do a thing. I think it will be up to a certain red-headed young man who seems to accept his challenges straight on. Look!"

At that, he pointed toward the sidewalk where, even as they were speaking, Sam walked by, escorting Inez on his arm.

"David has gone to fight his Goliath," Arthur chuckled and William nodded consent.

The stroll had been Inez' idea. Without William and Arthur in the house, poor Sam seemed at odds as to what to do with himself. She could tell he felt awkward with girl talk going on and nothing to do. As much as she hated to admit it to herself yet, she was quite taken with him physically. She remembered what it was like to be a young girl, and could see why Victoria was infatuated with him. So, deciding to take the bull by the horns, she began, "Samuel, this is no place for a young man, and I feel the need to get some fresh air. Could you escort me, please?"

Welcome relief flooded over Sam to have a reason to get away from girlish chatter, but his knees also went weak at the thought of a direct confrontation so soon with the one person whom he knew would hold every word he said in judgment. With a deep breath and a quick prayer, he said, "Yes, ma'am. It would be my distinct pleasure."

He helped her with her hat and shawl and they exited the house. "I'm sorry that I'm unfamiliar with the town and which way to go, ma'am, but if you'll take my arm I'll gladly take you wherever you wish to go."

Inez couldn't help but notice that his speech was exceedingly polite and gram-matically perfect. She couldn't help but comment on it. "Samuel, do you always speak in this manner?"

"I'm not sure what you mean, ma'am."

"Your diction is crisp, your enunciation is clear, and your etiquette is flawless. Do you understand that?"

"Yes, ma'am. I pride myself in reading as often as I can get my hands on a book. I love to learn new things and feel that a day wouldn't be complete without having learned something new. As for the rest, well, I also try to be a Southern gentleman, ma'am, for I feel that if you can't pride yourself on manners and speech, you are no better off than the swine. Excuse my analogy, ma'am."

Inez caught herself smiling. "Samuel, I quite agree. Manners and speech are what set a man aside from the common riff raff from the street. All men, I should think, have dreams and goals. All men have talents and natural abilities, but it is what one does with them that causes some to rise above others. It is initiative and hard work. Do you agree, Samuel?"

"Yes, ma'am. I have no aspirations to be a government leader, for example, but I have a great desire to provide a good life for myself and my family, to stretch myself mentally and physically above where I started out in life, to love and be loved." Sam said this last phrase without thinking about it. After it came out, he caught his breath quickly, fearing he may have let on too suddenly and too emo-tionally his desire to marry this woman's daughter, but Inez seemed to be caught up in a great dream of her own.

"My own dear husband feels quite as passionately as you about the same things. He has often said, 'Hard work, solid convictions, and a backbone in adversity. That's what makes a man.' I haven't always shared his sentiments in all aspects of life, for you see, I was raised in a life of leisure. My grandfather owned a shirt factory in the North before the Civil War. Before the War, he did well, very well, for himself. The war, though, about ruined us. Cotton, of course being a main stay of the Southern economy, was difficult to find for a while. But my grandfather and then my father after him, both found people in the South willing to trade with us. They had cotton. We had money. About 25 years ago my father introduced one of the first shirt factories in New York City. It was a shrewd busi-ness move. Cheap help from all the immigrants, mostly Irish and some Polish, was easily available. We prospered for a long while. My family often took trips to the cotton plantations and mills in Southern Virginia and Northern North Caro-lina. In fact, that is how I met William. His family was one of the main providers of our cotton. Well, as you may or may not know, there have been some problems in our industry. The fire at the Triangle Shirt Factory, our major competitor, taught us all a few things about the changing times. My father, always being one to resist change, fought the unions until he was no longer able to. It was either that or lose the business. So he conceded. All he ever wanted was to do better than his father and to provide a good life for his family. And he did. Each of us married well and have been able to enjoy some of life's luxuries. We recently installed a telephone in our house, for example. That is something he never would have dreamed imaginable."

At that, Inez caught herself and realized that they had walked and talked for a number of blocks. As she looked up, she noticed that she and Samuel were on the main street of town, facing the docks and the bay. Slightly embarrassed that she had revealed so much about her family history to this stranger, she reddened slightly and said, "Oh, but I'm sure that is all terribly uninteresting to you."

"No, ma'am. I would like to know more about your family. I already know quite a bit about your husband and his side of the family from the stories that Arthur has told, but it would help me to get to know you better, ma'am, if you don't mind."

Feeling quite at ease on this simply polite young man's arm, Inez felt herself relaxing and giving in to him. Later she would wonder if Victoria felt similarly, but for now she continued, "Well, as for myself and William, we met and married after a whirlwind courtship. He was so dashing and so romantic. His family had the plantation, they were well bred and well reared, and life seemed to promise him many good things. So we married. He has always been a good provider, even though he chose to give up everything on the plantation and come to New York with me. His business head far exceeds that of most. I think it is because he has a knack for dealing with people. He genuinely likes people and is one of those who would give the shirt off his back for a friend in need. We have always had plenty and we have been richly blessed with two sons and Victoria. They are all healthy, intelligent, and have their father's good sense and people skills. The boys will help their father with the business for as long as they wish, probably jointly running it after he leaves it to them. As for Victoria, I don't know. Choices for women of good breeding are limited in this day and age, as you know."

Then, fearing she had offended him, she quickly added, "No offense to you or yours, of course."

"None taken, ma'am." Sam chuckled as he realized how she rambled on sometimes without thinking of how her words might affect others. Then, as they turned onto the street where the Brittanhaur house was located, she began again.

"I have prattled long enough about myself and now I see that we are nearly home. Will you promise me another stroll tomorrow morning? Right now I am feeling a little tired from the day's excitement, but tomorrow I should like to know more about you. Is that fair?"

"Oh, yes, ma'am. I will earnestly look forward to then," he replied with a relieved grin.

Inez looked into his face as he held the wrought iron gate open for her. She couldn't help but smile back at him. His child-like innocence, his open honesty, and his youthful optimism struck her as unusually becoming. "Yes," she had to admit to herself, "he is a very likeable young man."

That evening after dinner found the whole family in the parlor of the pristine Victorian home. They were enjoying some parlor games, with the girls going between fits of laughter and moments of seriousness while trying to impress Sam with their knowledge. He, for his part, was not to be out done, and managed to hold up his end of witty pursuits quite well. It was obvious from the look in her eyes that Victoria wished to spend time alone with him, but she had to admit that, as a family, they all had a wonderful evening laughing and playing together.

The next morning, after breakfast, William and Arthur excused themselves from the rest of the family, claiming to have some important family business to take care of. With only women left for entertainment again, Sam felt lost, wishing something needed repairing, replacing, or at the very least, some attention. But the house was in perfect condition. Not used to a life of relaxation, he thought about asking to go fishing, but just then Inez caught his attention.

"Well, now, Samuel, I must say that eating this heavily and doing nothing is testing my constitution. I suspect you feel the same."

"Yes, ma'am," he began, "I could sure use something physical to do."

"Then it is time for another walk," she declared.

Victoria's eyes caught Sam's with a pleading look of "When are we ever going to have time alone together?" but sensing the importance of winning her mother's approval, she smiled and teased, "My goodness, mother. You and Sam are spending so much time together! Are you sure Daddy won't be jealous?"

"Victoria, you may have your chance this afternoon while we all go to the beach for a lovely outing, but for now, the outing won't even transpire unless I am perfectly satisfied with every element of this man." Inez was often blunt to the point of being abrasive, especially with those closest to her.

Bristling in response, Victoria acquiesced with a quiet, "Yes, mother."

Sam, too, shuddered with the magnitude of the conversation that he and Inez were about to embark on. He feared that one wrong word would doom the future he so earnestly desired.

"Here we go, then," Inez said slightly more cheerfully to Sam as he helped her with her wrap and held the door open for her. "We will see you all later. Good-bye."

Sam threw one last desperate glance over his shoulder as he shut the door behind him. Looking dreadfully like a sheep being led to the slaughter, Verna commented, "I hope she's not too rough on the boy. I do like him so!"

"Alright, now, Samuel," Inez began as they stepped onto the sidewalk. "It is time for you to tell me about your family. Be perfectly honest and open. A lot rides on this conversation."

"Yes, ma'am." Sam started. At first his words came hesitantly as if he were searching for just the right words to say to impress her, but as he went on he forgot about impressing her and was more intent on telling the story of his father in the Civil War, his family and their hardships with farming, and his current life at Arthur's plantation. When his history reached the current years, Inez finally interrupted him.

"Samuel, tell me how you and Victoria met, please, and how intimate, I mean close, you two have become."

Samuel told her everything from his perspective, including how he felt when he first saw Victoria, how he had grown fond of her over the years during her visits at Arthur's plantation, and how he appreciated her naive view of the world. He told Inez how he longed to protect her, to see that her dreams of the world were never tarnished, and to help her accomplish her goals for her life. As he finished, he sighed, and said, "Thank you, Mrs. Brittanhaur, for this time to tell you the things of my heart that maybe even Victoria doesn't know."

"Samuel," she replied, discreetly wiping away a tear, "You are a most honorable man. Never have you mentioned selfish things. You think of others and how life will be for them. You go to extremes to right the wrongs of the world. You are not the typical young person, thinking that the world was made for them and them alone. Samuel, I am touched by your openness and sincerity shown to an old lady."

The late morning hours Sam spent with Victoria, preparing for the family outing. They were supervised by Verna, who kept them rather busy, but always managed to send the two of them out of the room for necessary items like a picnic basket or a table cloth.

"Finally!" Victoria exclaimed as she grasped Sam's hand on the way toward the linen closet in the back of the house. "You've been here over 24 hours and I haven't had time to speak to you alone at all!"

Sam chuckled. Had it been only 24 hours? It seemed like an eternity to him. "Virdie," he started quite seriously. "I have had a chat with your father and two long walks and talks with your mother. I can't imagine what the two of them think of me and what they are doing right now."

It was true. Inez had finished their walk in a rather cryptic manner, saying she had had enough walking and needed to speak to her husband. The two of them were upstairs in their bedroom, very quiet. It made Sam nervous, as if the fate of his whole life depended on two people judging him after a short time, but then he remembered the moment at hand.

"Well, your Aunt Verna is sly for sending us on errands together. She makes it seem so natural-you know where the things are, but I'm needed to lift them down or carry them. She's fancies herself quite a match maker, I think!" At this he chuckled and shook his head at the odd variety of personalities in this family. Having found what they were after, Sam quickly grabbed Victoria and held her to him. The hug turned into a rather lengthy kiss, which was interrupted when they heard footsteps coming from the kitchen. Victoria reddened as Cousin Sarah came through the doorway.

"Hi! There you two are. Mother was wondering if you were having trouble finding the pickles. She told me to tell you she would have put them on the back of the shelf up high. You know she's not fond of them but knows everyone else is."

Sam and Victoria just looked at each other and grinned with a secret hidden better than pickles and followed Sarah back to the kitchen.

On the beach that afternoon, nine people laughed and played in the sand. Inez and Verna, from having been reared in an era when it was improper for a lady to show her ankles and to have light skin was desirable, stayed in the protection of the few loblolly pine trees and their umbrellas. The girls, however, took off their shoes and socks and frolicked in the sand, contenting themselves to make sand castles after the initial newness wore off. The three men decided to walk out onto the pier to fish. As many men do, they sat there for over an hour, not saying a word, except to comment on each others' catches when they were hauled in. As it turned out, Sam could have won the award for best fisherman for the day. He caught twice as many as the older men put together.

"Now, Sam," William began with a teasing grin, "You really must share with me your secret for catching fish."

"Sir, there's no secret, but I do come from a fishing family. Maybe it's just in my blood!

The men bantered that idea around for a little while, then decided that they had enough for a meal and returned to the shore to start a fire on the beach. The evening meal turned out to be a feast of sorts, with fresh flounder and blue fish, sweet potatoes roasted in the fire, fresh cherries picked from a neighbor's tree by the younger girls, and, of course, pickles.

"This is great!" exclaimed Mary and Margaret together.

"Yes," Verna agreed, "I don't recall when was the last time I ate fish that tasted this good!"

"Thanks to Sam." Arthur chimed in. "He's quite the fisherman. William and I are jealous of him right now. He won't share his fishing secrets with us."

Sam reddened and the family all laughed good naturedly. Sam could see that this easy banter was just a way that they showed affection toward each other and he was glad to be included in it.

As the party made their way toward home, Sam and Victoria finally had a little time together. They lagged behind the rest of the group to talk, but Sam felt awkward as his hands were laden with a picnic basket and fish poles.

"You've spent a lot of time with my family the last few days," Victoria began. "What do you think of them?"

"Your father is so much like his brother that it's uncanny. They both dote on all you girls and give you everything you want. He even treats your mother that way. I'm not sure I could ever live up to the standards he has. As for your mother, well, we have talked a lot. I like her. I think she's cautious on your behalf. She just wants your happiness, but, Virdie," here he paused for a slight moment, "I'd really like to have the chance to prove to her that I can be a good provider for you."

Realizing that they had very few moments together when they could talk, Victoria slowed her step a little and looked at Sam more directly.

"Sam, are you asking me to marry you?"

"No," he stuttered, then "Yes, well, no, I mean. There you go again. See what affect you have on me? You turn me into a babbling idiot!"

He took a deep breath and started again. "I want to ask your father first for your hand in marriage. I want to do everything properly, everything right by your 'high society' ways."

Victoria stopped and stared at him. "What do you mean by 'my' high society ways? All that facade of fancy this and fancy that means nothing to me. You know that. You know that I would give up everything I ever had, ever was, or ever dreamed of being just to be with you." She stopped, realizing that her voice had gotten louder and faster.

The rest of the group had gratefully continued walking, although because it was getting dark it was getting hard to see where they were.

Now it was Sam's turn to tease a little, "So does that mean you'd say 'yes' if I were proposing?"

Victoria's whole countenance changed as she leaned against him ever so slightly and looked straight into his blue eyes. "Yes, Sam, a thousand times yes. And the sooner the better!"

"You might regret those words, Miss Brittanhaur," he teased a little more.

But not to be outdone, she answered with, "And so may you, Mr. Harrell."

At that, they kissed. Not a long, lingering, passionate kiss, but a quick, affectionate, and playful kiss that represented the relationship they had established as friends first, then lovers. Then they hurried on to catch up to the rest of the group, who seemed not to have missed them at all as they chattered and laughed their way home.

The next day William and Arthur discussed traveling north to see the hotel they had both invested in. Called Hotel Wachapregue after the name of the city it was located in, they both hoped the projected four story building would become a great resort on the Eastern Shore and draw lots of tourists. The hotel, advertised as being one of the most elaborate for miles around, would serve a very elite clientele. But after looking on a map, they decided against the trip as it was their last day together, or so they thought. Instead, they decided that the well needed some repair. Sam was glad to be at something physical again and enjoyed his time working with the Brittanhaur brothers. When Arthur went back into the pantry to fetch some more tools, Sam took the opportunity to ask William if he could speak to him in private when they had the chance. The older man easily consented, suspecting the content of the future conversation.

It wasn't until after lunch that the two men had a chance to chat, feigning the excuse of needing a few more nails. So they headed west toward Main Street, just one block away.

They found the supplies they needed at Hopkins and Brothers, Inc., a local establishment that was known for its trading and shipping. If they didn't have something, it was likely it wasn't to be had in this community. On the way back, Sam knew he had to initiate his conversation or lose the chance.

"Sir, I need to address something quite personal with you, and having never done this before, I'm not quite sure where to begin," he began in a rush of words.

"It's alright, Sam, I think I know what you want and you have my full permission to continue."

"Thank you, Sir." He took a deep breath and continued. "I love your daughter and believe she loves me. I want nothing more in life than to provide her with a good home and to protect her with all my heart and soul." That said, he looked into the eyes of the older man. Surprised, he saw one of the biggest grins he had ever seen. "Sir? Do you find this funny?"

"Oh, no, son. It's just that I have grown so fond of you over the last few days and so impressed with you and with what Arthur has told me about you, that I was hoping you would suggest marriage. I think Victoria is a very lucky young lady."

"Thank you, Sir. But as for Mrs. Brittanhaur?"

William smiled and said, "Let me tell you how we are going to handle her. You and I are going to pretend that this conversation never happened." He saw Sam's look of concern and quickly continued, "Then, after we are done with this well project, request to speak to her and me in the parlor privately. There you may ask for our daughter's hand in marriage from the both of us at the same time. I, of course, will give my consent. She may be surprised and drag her feet a little, but leave that up to me. Don't be surprised at anything I say or do. Alright?"

Sam replied with more than a little concern, "Yes, Sir, thank you, Sir."

That afternoon Sam did exactly as he was told. He took a moment after finishing with the well to wash his hands and face, comb his hair, and brush his teeth. Then he requested the appointment. His knees shook as he walked in to find Mr. and Mrs. Brittanhaur seated closely side by side on a new Victorian love seat.

William initiated the conversation and Sam knew he was trying to put him at ease.

"There, Sam, pull up that chair near us and tell us what's on your mind, son."

Sam noted the term of affection and imagined that William was orchestrating a great affair as easily as he would a treaty between two great nations.

"Mr. and Mrs. Brittanhaur, over the last two years I have become very fond of your daughter. In fact, I have grown to love her more than any other on the face of this earth. Therefore, I respectfully request your permission to marry her." It came out a lot faster than he had planned, and this dismayed him.

The elderly couple didn't budge. Not a muscle seemed to move in either one's face. Then William reached over and took his wife's hand and said, "This is not unexpected, Sam, in light of the last few days. We have noticed Victoria's fondness for you and are refreshed by the good report of you by my brother and his family. Therefore, young man, I say 'Welcome to the family!'"

Inez seemed to color somewhat at the readiness that William had to give his daughter away. She started to protest, but William cut her off. "Oh, dear, isn't it exciting? Another wedding in our family! And I can't think of a finer man in all of New York City!"

Inez, finally finding her voice, started to protest, "But William, they are so young. They…"

But again he cut her off. "Now, dearest, remember that you and I knew each other less than a year before we were married. Remember what that felt like? Oh, we should thank our Heavenly Father for his gracious provision for our daughter."

"But his life style is nothing like ours and…" Inez' mind was racing with a myriad of excuses to not lose her daughter.

"Dear," William said in a firmer tone of voice, "what is important to you and me isn't necessarily important to young people these days. Don't you remember your father saying something similar when I took you away to the big city?"

She paused, knowing that his mind was made up and that as head of the household he would have the last say. She knew she often said her piece even when she shouldn't and had more freedoms and input in their marriage than many of her peers did, but she knew when to stop and keep quiet, also. She also wondered why she was really putting up any resistance. She truly liked this gentlemanly young man. Even though he wasn't from a rich, society family, there was something about him that was most engaging. She felt warm and comfortable around him. She felt like she could trust him with anything. "Even her daughter?" she wondered to herself. "Yes, even her daughter."

William, recognizing his upper hand and that the battle was won, stretched out his hand and said, "Congratulations, son, you're getting a fine young woman for your wife."

Shaking his future father-in-law's hand with sincere appreciation, Sam said, "Yes, Sir, I know, Sir." Then he turned to Inez and got down on his knees in front of her. "Ma'am, I will do my best to provide for your daughter well. We may not have the luxuries that she is accustomed to, but we will never go hungry and we will never lack for love or laughter in our home."

Inez, her heart melting with the realization that this young man truly knew what was important in life, smiled resignedly, and stretched out her hand also. "Yes, Samuel, I know you will do your best."

"Then I have your blessing, Ma'am?"

"Yes, Samuel, you do."

At that, he kissed her hand as gently and sincerely as he had done the first day they met, and as he looked up to meet her eyes, they each noticed that tears were near to over-flowing.

At that precise moment, Arthur and Verna entered the parlor and shut the pocket doors behind them.

"So here you all are. We've been wondering what was going on," Arthur teased good naturedly.

William was the one to break the good news, and as if caught up in a whirlwind that he had no control over, Sam sat off to one side of the two couples as they planned the next few days of his life for him. It was Arthur who suggested that they have the wedding immediately.

"Why not?" he asked in all seriousness. "We're all together, and how often does that happen?"

Verna confirmed that they could all take the ferry across to Sunbury in the morning, that by afternoon they could contact their minister, who she was confident could come to the house the next day and perform the ceremony. "Of course we won't have time, Inez, to furnish the girls with fancy dresses or an elaborate setting, but the important thing is that the young people will be surrounded by their family."

Sam started to protest that he couldn't possibly find a place for himself and Victoria to live in such a short time, but Arthur solved that problem in his typically generous way. "Verna, as our wedding gift to the couple, let's give them the house on the north end of the plantation. William, what do you say? You know the plantation was your home at one time, too, and I still feel that it partly belongs to you."

"Arthur, that is a very generous offer. Being the business man I am, I would say we should draw up a contract to the effect that they own the house and the surrounding 10 acres for as long as they live there. But I feel that, in order to keep our end of our dear father's will, we must add a proviso that, heaven forbid, in the event of death or divorce the house and land revert back to you. Agreed?"

Arthur and William, who seemed to know more of the complicated workings of some document foreign to their wives and Sam, were agreed. And so it was, that rather than return to New York the following day, William, Inez, and Victoria wired for the rest of the family to join them as soon as possible at Sunbury and all nine of them took the steamer across the bay the following morning.

The rest of the day was spent getting everyone settled in at the plantation house and the William Brittanhaur family meeting the Javan Harrell family. Javan and Ann seemed cautious and surprised. Perhaps they were thinking of the large undertaking their son was embarking on. William felt that surely Javan must have as many doubts and questions as Inez, but he and Ann came to a quiet agreement that everything would work out just fine.

Victoria's brother Edward and his wife and baby were able to get away from the business because of the up-coming fourth of July holiday. Paul, who helped in the family business also, was glad to get away and do something exciting. They all rode the train to Cape Charles that day and took the steamer across the next morning. The wedding took place that afternoon, July 3, 1901.

Aunt Verna had decked the porches of Sunbury with cuttings from the magnolia trees and swatches of cloth tied into bows. The Episcopalian minister that had served the Brittanhaur family for years, literally in sickness and in health, in good times and in bad, performed the simple but elegant ceremony. Everyone wore their best clothes, and Sam was particularly glad to have a new suit available for the occasion. The ladies dabbed at their eyes at how happy the couple seemed to be, and as the minister finished with his sermonette about love and commitment, Sam turned to his bride, took her hand in his, whispered, "I love you. I will always love you." and kissed her. The crowd burst into cheering and clapping.

A meal followed on the back lawn under the shade of some old magnolia trees. Aunt Verna had thought of every detail for a feast. A hog had been butchered, all sorts of fresh berries, jams, jellies, canned vegetables from the year before, and breads of every imaginable sort spread across tables moved out for the feast. Aunt Verna had even sent some of the servants the day before to clean and polish the house that was to become home for the newlyweds. So as the sun set in the west, the couple retired to their own home, the place they would live for all their married life.

The next day saw more tears than the day before. William, Inez, Edward, his wife and baby, and Paul all needed to return to the city before Monday of next week when a new work week began. They planned to go across as far as Cape

Charles that day and continue the trek north by train the day after that. That would give them one day to relax and rest before beginning work again. As they said their good-byes, Victoria kissed each one and was kissed by each one. Sam held her hand gently, knowing these last few days had been a whirlwind of emotions and activity for them both. But now she was to lose some of the most familiar things to her. He understood her feelings and vowed to be there for her. He shook hands with her brothers then went to shake hands with her mother.

"Take good care of my baby, Samuel," she said, choking back tears.

"I promise you to do my best, Ma'am." he responded in all seriousness.

"Samuel?" Here she paused. "May I call you Sam?" she asked, and as he nodded his assent, she continued, "and now, in light of things, you may call me Inez, or Mother Brittanhaur, or something a little less formal than 'ma'am.'"

"Thank you, ma…., I mean, Inez. I appreciate that." They both smiled at each other.

Last to shake his hand was William. "Congratulations, son." was all he said, but his hand shake spoke a thousand words. Then he turned to his daughter. "Honey, make him happy. He is a good man, remember that."

"Yes, Daddy," she replied, and then he climbed into the buggy and they all waved as the horses trotted down the driveway.

Left alone, they waved till the buggies were no longer in sight, then the couple began the walk to their house. Their home. Their own nest. Arm in arm they went, to celebrate the birth of our nation as only newlyweds can.

"Good morning, wife," Sam said gently.

Victoria opened her eyes and realized it wasn't even light out yet. "Why are you up so early?" she moaned.

"Because I have to go to work. What are you going to do today?" he replied.

"I don't know. What should I do?" she asked, truly puzzled as she was unused to needing to do too much for herself. She had realized over the last few days how much had been done for her before.

"May I suggest you go see my mother? Maybe ask her how to make biscuits or something. She's a really good cook."

More awake now, Victoria decided to tease the poor man. "Does that imply that I'm not?" she said in a defensive tone.

Knowing she was teasing, Sam took the bait, "Oh, of course not, my dear, it just implies that we needn't go into the brick business as there are several other flourishing ones in the area!"

Then they tickled each other, and teased, and played until Sam noticed that the sun was coming up. "I've got to go. Your Uncle Arthur will be disappointed if I'm not on time, and we mustn't disappoint him after all he has done for us." With that he got up, dressed and was almost out the door when he called back to her, "Do you hear your birds this morning? I think they're louder than ever now that you're here."

She laid in bed and listened for a little while. Yes, the birds were all tuned up this morning, greeting a new day full of fresh dreams and new hopes.

Victoria's day that day became like many that year. She would do the little things that needed to be done around their home. Then she would walk down to her mother-in-law's house. The ten acres around their house had been planted in June, so the arrangement between Sam and Uncle Arthur was that the couple would get half the profit from those ten acres. With that they would be able to buy their own seed for planting next year and then whatever they made off the land would be completely theirs. As for a garden, this year they didn't have one of their own. It was really too late to plant by the time they were married, so Vicky went to help Ann and Javan in theirs. It turned out to be a real blessing both ways.

Walt had decided he needed a profession that he could do on his own with only one good eye and one good arm. In the newspaper he had read about a photographer in Ohio who took apprentices for a year and trained them in the business. Their schooling was in exchange for their help with the business. So Walt had gone off to learn what he felt was a business that could only prosper.

Javan and Ann missed Walt around the house. He had always been a good helper to them, but now Vicky was there to take his place. Both parents became fond of her quickly. She was eager to learn and always pleasant to be around, but sometimes they had to wait till she had gone home before they could chuckle over some comment or question during the day. Surely she was the most naive thing they had ever run across. Both of them were from common stock, and they knew what hard work was like. To Vicky, even hoeing in the garden was an adventure. Figuring out which was a weed and which was a good plant was a source of concern for her. All those things that came naturally to them from years of practice, they now saw through the eyes of a novice. But she never took offense at her lack of knowledge of practical things. She would just laugh, make some funny comment that put them all at ease, and go on.

Ann was able to put her to work in the garden by herself rather quickly. She showed her how to cook, how to sew, how to mend and darn, how to butcher a chicken, how to put up the vegetables from the garden so they would have good food all winter, and how to be frugal when it comes to household things such as using wash water to scrub the floors.

The hours the two women spent together were good ones. They became so fond of each other that Victoria found she would rather spend the day with Ann, quilting on a cool winter's day in her humble cottage rather than at Sunbury chatting with her cousins and being waited on. Sundays, though, were different. Sam's family had not been raised to be particularly religious. Although Sam was, the couple found that it was very enjoyable and a great compromise to spend Sundays in a routine way. They would wash up and put on their best clothes, walk over to the plantation, then ride to church in the buggy with Uncle Arthur and Aunt Verna. Afterward they would return to a large lunch laid out by the household servants. After that, the servants were dismissed until Monday. They did whatever they pleased for the rest of the day, and the family snacked on leftovers or fended for themselves for dinner. As time went on, Victoria became more adept at fixing left overs into an appetizing dish.

Sometimes the ladies would spend the afternoon just sitting and chatting, but that made Victoria feel guilty. She knew Sunday was a day of rest, but she felt that it was a reversion to her old way of life rather than her new way of life. She preferred to be busy, even if it meant quietly sitting in the parlor with the rest of the family but stitching or quilting while they chatted.

Aunt Verna, remembering what it was like to be a newlywed and wanting to please a husband, allowed Victoria the freedom to come and go as she wished. She enjoyed their time together immensely, knowing that soon her own girls would be married and gone and then the big house would feel that much larger. She sought solace in the fact that Victoria, at least, was within walking distance. Then, too, she remembered the lean times from when she and Arthur were first married. So it was that when Victoria did come to visit, she often tried to get her to take back some canned food or tidbits from the table that the family had for dinner the day before. Aunt Verna, watching the transformation of Victoria over the course of time, discovered that she was becoming quite an independent, self-sufficient housewife. And, without ever saying so, she was impressed. She was sure her girls would never survive under similar circumstances and she wondered if she had done them wrong by bringing them up in a household of luxury.

One evening as the sun was setting, Sam and Virdie sat on their porch, rocking. She, of course, was listening to the birds. Sam was lost in his own reverie. Suddenly, he broke the silence.

"I've got it," he snapped. "We'll call our home 'Bird's Nest.'"

Victoria was lost as to where this outburst came from or was going. "Sam, what are you talking about?"

Realizing she didn't understand what he was referring to, he explained.

"All the big plantations have fancy names. The old ones on up the James River are Berkeley and Shirley and Evelynton. Some are named for people. Some are named for an aspect of area, like Oakton, Duckington, and Holly Grove. Others are purely fictional, like Sunbury. So I think we should name our place 'The Bird's Nest.'"

Victoria chuckled at how whimsical her husband could be. "Is our little home large enough to warrant a fanciful name like that?" she asked, playfully.

He smiled back at her, "Not yet, but hopefully it will be some day. We have plenty of birds, and our little home is our first nest. For you, oh bird lover Virdie, it is fitting name."

With that said, it was official. "The Bird's Nest" belonged to them and it suited them both perfectly.

In the summer of 1902, Walt returned from Ohio. He was so excited to start his new profession that he borrowed some money to set up a studio in downtown Suffolk. He convinced his younger brother Ben to join him, mostly as an apprentice, but also as a partner once he had been trained, if he decided he liked the business. The two boys, now men, who had always been close, decided to move into an apartment above the studio to save the expense of traveling back and forth every day.

It was at this time that Victoria became even more precious to Ann and Javan. With their home devoid of children except for James, they found themselves anxiously awaiting her arrival each day. She became a caring and loving daughter to them, even to the point of surprising them with little gifts she made for them and anticipating needs they had, emotionally and physically. Sometimes her gifts were nothing more than some wild flowers she picked on her way there, but Ann, who was unaccustomed to the attentions of another woman, totally adored her thoughtfulness. To both women the days seemed long when they were unable to be together for at least some time.

The farm did well. One by one Victoria's cousins were married to local plantation owner's sons or businessmen from the city. Little by little it seemed that Sam and Victoria became more important and more relied upon by Uncle Arthur as his girls moved away. Frank, the old foreman, and Sam practically ran the whole plantation now, choosing to do much of the work themselves rather than hire others to do it. They worked long, hard hours, but were well rewarded for it.

In the Spring, Sam would help Vicky plant a garden near their home. In the summer and fall she tended it and made good use of every part of nature's bounty. Ann had taught her well and Vicky took to her chores with an eagerness to do her best to be a contributing member of their family.

By this time Sam's brother Richard and his wife, Mary Ann, had decided to move back to the area. They had been trying to be farmers in Nansemond County, but weren't successful at it. With the help of Javan, Richard was set up as a grocer in nearby Suffolk. Javan would take extra produce from the gardens to him and Richard would sell it to the city people. This venture turned out to be quite profitable for all involved, which eventually included even Arthur.

It was after the harvest was in for the year 1903. The crop was a good one and Sam found that they had a little money to spare, even after setting plenty aside for seed and help for the next year. So, one cool morning in the first part of December, he asked Victoria, "How would you like to go spend Christmas with your parents?"

"You're kidding, right?" she inquired.

"No. I'm serious. We have some extra money and right now there's nothing to do around the farm. We could take a week or two off and go visit them. You've worked so hard here that you deserve a break. I know you must miss them and you never say anything about it or complain any, so I just wanted to give you a treat."

"Will your folks be alright by themselves for the holidays? You know how alone they are now that all the boys have gone." Victoria's fondness for Ann in particular made her concern a vital one. James had recently moved in with Walt and Ben in town, as the boys were prospering at their photography studio and had needed a bookkeeper. James seemed to enjoy the job and did it well, always having been one with a constitution more suited for indoor jobs than outdoor.

Sam reassured her that they could have an early holiday with his parents and then leave to make it to New York by Christmas Day.

"Great! Let's do that! Should we surprise them or wire them that we're coming?"

"Let's wire them. I suspect your mother isn't much of one for surprises."

Vicky chuckled, "You're right there! She could hardly stand her birthday or Christmas for not knowing what the gifts under the tree were that Daddy put there. Speaking of gifts, what will we take them?"

Sam, ever the practical one, commented, "Isn't it enough for us to be there?"

Yes, he was right, but she still wanted to take something. So she looked through the pantry and decided that her own bread and butter pickles would be a treat. Surely her Mom would be impressed that she could do this for herself.

The decision was made. They would leave the following Saturday. Uncle Arthur would take them as far as the bay where they would take the steamer across and the train to New York. Sam, having never ridden a train before, was a little anxious about that part of the trip, but Victoria assured him that once he rode one, he would always want to ride one. She found the powerful engines to be terribly fascinating, just as she did many things in her child-like way. So Sam kissed her, appreciating her strength, her enthusiasm, and her love of life.

Once in New York, Sam was amazed and felt dwarfed by the tall buildings that seemed to surround him on every side. Almost feeling claustrophobic, he coughed at the air that smelled of coal oil, dirt, and city that had seen four inches of snow already. The couple got off the train and found a cabby to take them to the great mansion that Victoria had called home. Sam was amazed again at the size of the house. Seeing a light on in every room, he exclaimed, "That must be some electric bill each month!"

"Mother wouldn't have it any other way on Christmas Eve." Victoria replied, "She thinks she has to outshine the neighbors in every conceivable way!"

The cab took them to the doorstep where they paid him and looked around the yard as the matched horses trotted off with the sleigh bells jingling merrily, spreading Christmas cheer and making the young couple smile despite their reluctance at entering this place of luxury.

Just then, the two large doors swung open and William stood with his arms wide open, saying, "Are you two going to stand there in the dark and cold or come inside for all of us to see you?"

"Daddy!" Victoria cried and jumped into his open arms.

"Sir." Sam followed, letting some of the bags down so that he could shake the older man's hand warmly.

"Now come in; come in. We were all beside ourselves wondering when you would get here. And now you're here! Oh, what a wonderful Christmas."

It was clear that the old gentleman was pleased to find his family back under his roof again, for there in the parlor were Edward, Susan, and little Evelyn, who was now three years old. She ran around the house non-stop with a tottering sort of gait that kept everyone on edge with fear that she might fall into some piece of furniture or another. But her most charming feature was that she would hold up her hands to be picked up by anyone and everyone, and once she was held, she would wrap her little fingers into the holder's hair and snuggle her little face against it.

Over the next few days, she discovered Uncle Sam to be her favorite. Even Susan commented on it, "I've never seen her take to anyone like she does to you, Sam. She wants you to hold her when she's hurt; she wants you to hold her when she's tired. I declare, you're just a natural with children."

Then Susan would turn her attention to Victoria. Not realizing that she was addressing a very personal issue, she asked, "And when are you two going to have children?"

Not quite knowing how to answer this blunt question, both Sam and Victoria blushed and stammered out something unintelligible.

But good old William came to the rescue. He hated to see anyone put into an awkward situation and quickly changed the subject for them. "Has everyone tasted these pickles? They are marvelous! And do you know what? Victoria made them all by herself. Here, have one." At this he passed around pickles that had been placed into one of her mother's dainty dishes. Victoria hated the fuss that was being made over simple little pickles, but appreciated her father for distracting the conversation from personal topics.

That evening, snuggled in the bed that she used to use as her own, Sam and Victoria whispered quietly to each other.

"Sam, you really are good with children. Evelyn adores you, you know."

"I'm fond of her, too. She is a pretty little thing with those brown eyes and that sweet smile. I could just sit and hold her for hours." he replied dreamily.

"Sam?" Victoria started and then stopped in a rather embarrassed fashion, glad that the lights were off and he couldn't see her face, "Do you want to have children?"

"Yes, of course, Virdie." he said, somewhat startled at her question, but understanding what had precipitated this conversation. "You know that I believe that children are a blessing from the Lord. When the time is right, He will give us the ones that are just right for us."

"Thank you, Sam. You're such a dear. I don't think I'll ever have the faith that you have. You see the world in such a.... well, bigger way than I do. And you're right. When we are meant to have children, we will. And for now, we'll just enjoy each other."

That's exactly what they did for the next hour.

The week flew by. Sam made sure to spend plenty of time with Inez, who was pleasant and easy to get along with now that her children were all within range. She had a wonderful holiday and commented with a foreboding of sadness that she thought it was the most memorable Christmas of her life and wondered aloud how many more there could possibly be for her. During the next few days she was fairly insistent on taking Victoria shopping for some new clothes. So the ladies went out and Sam was left in the house with the servants. William and the boys had gone back to work at the family business.

The immenseness of the house distracted Sam. It was true that the electric lights and heat were quite convenient. His own mother, he thought, would love the linoleum floor in the kitchen that was so easy to clean up. But the lavishness compared to what he was used to made him feel awkward. He thought that even the house servants felt more at home than he did. He couldn't help but wonder if Victoria missed all this luxury and he regretted not being able to supply her every whim. But then, he scolded himself, she had never complained about the lack of luxury in their home. Feeling confused, Sam felt that maybe some fresh air would do him good, so he put on his hat and coat and went outside for a look around. He noticed the lack of birds, as Victoria had often commented on. He noticed the bare trees, the dirty snow on the ground, and the starkness of the city. People seemed to pass by in a big hurry. They didn't seem to have time to stop to visit or even say hello. He wondered if they were all sad because they didn't have contact with each other. He realized that the people of her neighborhood may have plenty of material possessions, but they lacked the two things he considered most important in his life: true love and a reason to live. Therefore, with his head feeling clearer, he decided he would appreciate Virginia and the plantation life even more when he returned.

At the end of his time of retrospection, Sam had to admit that Victoria's family had made him feel welcome and that the train trip north had been one of the most exciting things he had ever done in his life. In fact, he remembered commenting to Victoria that riding trains was something he thought he could do every day and never get tired of. The entire Brittanhaur and Harrell family would look back on this Christmas many years later with the hindsight that comes so clearly while looking at the past and realize that many events that take place and words that are spoken become prophecies of things to come all too soon.

The last evening that Sam and Victoria were to spend in New York, William and Inez (although it was mostly Inez) decided to take them to a fancy restaurant for dinner. Inez was terribly excited about just the four of them going.

"This is one of the best places in all New York to eat, Samuel," she told him as they bounced along in the cab on streets made uneven from snow hiding the intricate system of pot holes.

Not really knowing what to say to this because he felt rather awkward about the whole thing, he replied, "I'm sure we'll have a lovely evening, Inez. Thank you for taking us."

Wanting to appear very posh, Inez told the rest of the party, "William and I will order for us all if you don't mind. We've eaten here before and we know what's good."

Knowing it was best and easiest to agree, they nodded and chattered on about trivial things. The waiter, dressed immaculately, came to the candle lit table and William simply pointed to an item on the menu. "We will all have this."

"Very good, Sir," the waiter said with not a change in facial expression.

After what seemed like a very long time to Sam, the food finally came. He recognized the dish immediately and grinned to himself at what Inez thought was so special. Eel.

"This is the specialty of the house," Inez continued her rave reviews of the restaurant, the staff and then the cook. "Only Pierre can cook eel like this! He's a genius when it comes to the culinary arts."

"Oh, I don't know, mother," started Victoria, not catching her husband's warning glance.

"Sam's mother cooks eel much better than this, I think."

Others around them didn't feel the immediate tension or see the downcast look on Inez' face.

"What? What do you mean, my dear?"

"Sam's brother Charlie is a fisherman. We all call him Captain Charlie. He catches many different types of fish and seafood, but he occasionally gets an eel. As he is not particularly fond of them and he says he doesn't have a ready market for them, he just brings them over to Javan and Ann. She fixes them up and calls us over because it's always too much food for just the two of them. I'm telling you, mother, she uses something that makes it taste ten times better than this."

Victoria hadn't meant to be hurtful to her mother, and now that the words were out of her mouth she realized that she had been. She had only meant to be complimentary toward Ann, and the exuberance of youth and new experiences clouded her social judgment.

"I'm sorry, mother. I didn't mean to hurt you."

William, always one to find the good in everything, said, "Victoria, you say that Captain Charlie can't find a market for his eels?"

"Yes, Daddy, there are so many in the bay now that they're almost pests, he says."

"Well, I think I have a new business venture on my hands." With that, William called the waiter to the table and asked to speak to the manager of the restaurant. The rest of the table sat, diverted from the previous uncomfortable situation, wondering what he was up to.

After a few moments the manager came over and began in a concerned tone, "I do hope everything is to your liking?"

"Yes, sir, the food is excellent, as always," William started. "But please have a seat for a moment. I have something to tell you."

After nearly a half hour of discussion with the manager and then the owner of the restaurant, an agreement was made. Captain Charlie had an outlet for his eels. William would be the manager of transportation and the restaurant would take all the eels that Charlie could catch, provided his mother's recipe was part of the initial shipment.

Sam shook his head in amazement as the party headed back to the Brittanhaur home. "I just never know what's going to happen next!" he exclaimed. "Not only did they let us have the whole meal on the house, Charlie's business will prosper besides!"

William smiled, patted Sam on the back, and thought to himself, "And it gives me good reason to come south to see my business interests…and my little girl…more often."

The following morning Sam and Victoria headed south on the New York, Philadelphia, and Norfolk Railroad. They went as far as Cape Charles, stayed overnight in the house there, and proceeded across the bay the following day, arriving at Sunbury by mid-afternoon. Uncle Arthur and Aunt Verna had greeted them at the dock and brought them home in their buggy. That had given them time to catch each other up on family happenings over the holiday.

As soon as they reached Sunbury, Sam and Victoria were anxious to go see Javan and Ann to tell them about the eel business. They, too, were excited about the prospect of advancing the business. While in Cape Charles, Sam had stopped by the "Pickle House." The wooden building was a factory of sorts, where clams were steamed, shucked, and hard-sealed in cans. Sam had talked to the owner and found that he was willing to take on added business with the canning of fish, seafood, and eels. He already had a thriving business because the building was a part of Magotha's Dock, also known as Ketcham's Dock for the builder John Whitman Ketcham. Being right on the bay, he had easy access north, south, and east. So he could be an integral part of the shipping of Charlie's eels, if everything went right.

Javan told Sam that Charlie and his family were planning to come by for dinner the following Sunday, so they could all plan to meet then. With the arrangements made and feeling rather tired from their exciting journey, Sam and Victoria were glad to get back to their humble abode.

CHAPTER 7

▼

THE FOREBODING

Within two months the Harrell family was prospering as it never had before. Charlie's fishing business had grown to the point where he hired help. Richard's produce stand had become a full fledged grocery store. Walt, Ben, and James were becoming well known photographers in the area, particularly with the wealthier people who had money to spend on such luxuries as portraits. Sam and Virdie were happier than they had ever imagined, and even Javan and Ann seemed to settle into a blissful contentment with all their children out of the house.

January and February of 1904 had come and gone. Partly due to a mild winter, the farmers and plantation owners were thinking of planting soon. As Sam sat in the evening looking over the Farmer's Almanac and seed books, he contented himself with his feet up by the fire.

"Virdie?" he started one evening, "Are you happy?"

"What a silly question! You know I am. I have never felt this sort of happiness before." She shook her head in disbelief as she continued her needlework by the fire. She had become quite good at several kinds of fancy stitching, due to Ann's careful tutelage, and now she was expanding her repertoire on pillowcases. Sam sometimes thought the fancy flowers and birds she embroidered on everything were frivolous, but if it made her happy and made her feel useful, then he was glad for it.

He thought about all his blessings: a warm, cozy home, a fulfilling job, a healthy family. But something seemed to gnaw at the back of his memory, something that he couldn't quite put his finger on.

"Virdie?" he started again, "Should we go see your parents again before planting starts?"

"What is bothering you tonight?" she questioned without answering his question first. "You seem so restless and concerned about something."

"I'm sorry. I was thinking of how many blessings we have and what a good life we have, but something keeps worrying me and I can't figure out what it is. What do you think?"

"There's nothing wrong. You're just anxious to get your hands and feet into the soil again and get the precious seeds into the ground. I declare I have never seen a man like you. All balled up into a knot when you have to be inside for any length of time. Sometimes I think you'd go out in a blizzard for no good reason just to get outside! I'm so glad we haven't had any terrible weather here. It's not like in New York where the snow can close down businesses and everything for several days."

"But back to my original question." he probed again. "Do you feel the need to go see your parents?"

"Well, not really," she admitted, "but I wouldn't mind getting away for a quick trip before planting starts. How about going to Cape Charles? Maybe Daddy and Mother could meet us there, if that would settle you down some."

"Yes. That's perfect!" he declared, with his heart already feeling lighter, "Can you wire them tomorrow?"

She agreed and he sat in front of the fire for only a little while longer while he dreamed of beans and corn and peanuts in neat rows and as tall as the sky. Then he went to bed.

Victoria, on the other hand, wondered what had bothered Sam so much. He was normally so calm, so easy going, and so resigned to the fact that God was in control that he didn't need to worry about anything. She couldn't get his words out of her head when she went to bed. So she lay there for a while, listening to the winter wind blow and branches brushing against the roof. She finally fell asleep, wishing the warm sun and summer birds were at their fullest around her.

The plans were made and it was the following Friday that Victoria and Samuel headed across the bay for a three day stay in Cape Charles. They met William and Inez Brittanhaur at the dock, the latter couple having arrived the day before.

"How were you able to get away for so long?" Victoria asked her father as they walked the few blocks to their house.

"Your brothers have such fine business heads on their shoulders that they really don't need me anymore," he replied with admiration in his voice.

"Oh, Daddy, we will all always need you," Victoria sighed, "You know that the only reason they do so well is because you trained them so well."

"That's right, William," Inez added. "You did a fine job in training all three children to have good business heads." By this time they were all in the house and Inez had unwrapped the gift Victoria had brought for her. It was a special gift for both of them-hand embroidered pillowcases. Inez hugged her daughter warmly. "Thank you, darling! These are too pretty to use. I'll put them..."

Victoria interrupted her, "No you don't! I made them for you to use. I want my handiwork to be near your head every single night as a reminder that I may be far away physically but not emotionally. Please, mother?"

"But, Victoria, what if I wear them out?"

"Oh, mother, really! If you wear them out or they get shabby from use in any way, I will make you more. Better ones. Prettier ones. As my skills improve, I will do that anyway. So please use them. Please?"

Inez conceded, "Yes, dear, I will. Thank you."

The four of them spent many happy hours together. All too soon their three days were at a close. The Brittanhaur's saw the Harrell's to the dock that Monday morning. They all waved good-bye to each other and watched until no longer able to see clearly as the ferry pulled away. On the trip home, Sam asked Victoria a very serious question.

"Virdie? Did your mother seem slower to you than normal?"

"What do you mean 'slower?'" she asked.

Sam tried to sound nonchalant, but the concern came out in his tone of voice. "She seemed to have to pause to think about what she was going to say before she said it. Sometimes I thought I caught her holding her head or shaking her head as if to clear it. Is she prone to headaches or such?"

Victoria paused a moment before she answered. "Well, my parents aren't getting any younger, you know. But, no, I really didn't notice anything pronounced. I think you're looking for something that's not there."

"Maybe so," Sam agreed, trying to convince himself that the inner gnawing was nothing.

They let the conversation drop as they held hands and watched one shoreline slip into the distance and another come into view.

The elder Brittanhaur's had enjoyed their trip to the beach so much and found that the business continued so well without William there to supervise, that they decided to make more use of their resort home. They attempted to visit once every two months, but the trips were sporadic. As it turned out, Arthur and Verna had just installed a telephone at Sunbury, so William would call his brother whenever he was able to head south. The two couples met at the resort town as often as possible.

CHAPTER 8

▼

THE DESTINY

It was during the summer after all the planting was completed that Sam and Victoria were able to make another trip to Cape Charles. Although their stay would only last a few days, they were excited to be making the trip again. Victoria had all kinds of news to tell her mother about her own garden she had planted this year and what her latest handicraft was. In fact, she had embroidered matching pillowcases for her father and mother that said "His" and "Hers." Victoria thought them quite elegant and Ann had praised her saying that her stitching on the back was just as fine as the front now. Coming from Ann, who was quite the handy person herself, this meant a lot to Vicky.

The evening of their first night there, William made up an excuse for himself and Sam to slip outside for a while. As the two men strolled down the street, William began.

"Son, I have something on my mind that I need to talk to someone about and I don't know who else to turn to."

"You know I would always help you in any way possible, Sir," Sam began, having never been able to lose the formality of terms that came from his up bringing.

"Yes, you're a good man and I know I can count on you. That's why I've come to you first." William continued, "Lately I've been noticing odd things about my wife."

"Odd, Sir? Like what?"

"Well, for example, the other night after dinner I found her in the kitchen putting all the silverware in her pockets. When I asked her what she was doing she commented, 'The squirrels would like some nuts.'"

"Was she joking around with you? Playing some game?"

Here William's voice almost sounded angry, "You know Inez better than that, young man! She never jokes around, particularly not with silver!"

Then he sighed and calmed down some. It was easy for Sam to tell from his tone of voice and the sag of the older man's shoulders that this was truly a heavy burden that he needed to share with someone.

"You're right, I'm sorry," Sam said quietly. "Sir, if I may be so bold as to ask have you taken her to a doctor yet?"

"No. She won't admit that anything is wrong. She says she's fine except for an occasional headache and she attributes that to growing older. She won't go. She hates doctors."

"If I may again be so bold to comment, Sir, but I have noticed this coming on for some time. In fact, I even mentioned it to Virdie, I mean Victoria, after our last visit over here. I noticed Inez then holding her head and shaking it sometimes as if to clear it. If she won't see a doctor because you ask her to, maybe she will if I do."

"Oh, thank you, Sam! I think she just might! You seem to have such a way with people. Please talk to her before you leave."

At that the two men patted each other's backs and went back into the house. Sam sighed, knowing that the gnawing feeling from the past had been some terrible foreshadowing of this unknown disease of his mother-in-law. For as much as other people saw her as a busy body or a socialite or any number of unpleasant things, he respected her and cared for her. He would do everything within his means to get her the care she needed.

"Inez? Could we go for a walk...like in the old days? Sam asked, followed by, "just you and me?"

"Well, now, it's been such a long time since a handsome young man asked me to go out with him that I hardly know how to respond!" she teased. Victoria always looked up in amazement at the way that only Sam could handle her mother. It was obvious that they each were quite fond of the other and the connection was beyond her comprehension, so she just smiled and shook her head.

Sam picked up Inez' shawl from the coat tree near the door and held the door for her as she stepped out. She took his arm and they walked along the now familiar streets.

"Tell me what's on your mind," Inez began without any preliminaries. It was so like her to be abrupt without intending to be mean, even when she was a strict adherent to social graces.

Sam wasn't sure how to begin, but took a deep breath and jumped right in, knowing that hedging any topic would serve no purpose with this lady.

"You know I'm very fond of you. I owe you so much. I don't ever want to see you hurting or hurt. I, oh Inez, I'm afraid there's something the matter." He stopped for a breath and Inez looked at him with a quizzical look.

"Are you well? Have you seen some change in Victoria?" she queried.

"No, Inez, please. This is very difficult. It's you." He stopped while she seemed to think for a moment.

"There's nothing wrong with me and you know it." came her curt reply.

Gathering all the boldness he had, he forged ahead.

"No, I don't know that. All I know is what I see and I see you hurting. You're having headaches more and more frequently. You are having trouble thinking straight sometimes. Words escape you. I don't know what else, but I know there is something the matter. Please, Inez, I don't want to lose you. Not if it can be helped. You need to help raise your grandchildren. I want you to see many more years of happiness. William needs you to share his retirement. He has worked hard all his life and he won't know how to be alone when he stops working. He needs you to be there for him. Your children need you. I need you. Please!"

He had said all that in such a rush because he was afraid that if he didn't those words would never be said. Not one for mushy sentiments, Inez would stop him if possible. Or so he thought. But she didn't. She didn't say a word. She just stood there facing him and finally a lone tear rolled down her cheek.

"You are so sweet." Then she collapsed in his arms, for once forgetting what anyone else watching might think. A flood gate seemed to have opened and she began to sob.

"I'm so afraid. Sometimes I wake up in the morning and don't know where I'm at," she began, "then I realize that I don't even know my own name. Sometimes I can't think of the right word to say or what it was I had intended to do next. I find myself out in the yard without a shawl and no reason for being there. Oh, Sam, is this just growing old? For if it is, I hate it. I don't feel like I know who I am anymore. I'm not me. I'm afraid I'm…. I'm scared, so scared. Please help me!"

Having said all this she paused to sob in his arms. He patted her shoulders and cooed comforting sounds as only he could do. Then he realized that she had lost weight and felt very bony and fragile beneath him.

"Come, let's go home." He slowly walked back alongside her, supporting most of her weight leaning against him. When they arrived, they went to the parlor and sat without discussing it. William and Victoria came in, having heard them arrive, and noticed that both had tears in their eyes. Sam and Inez sat side by side on the Victorian love seat that graced the windowed side of the room.

Sam, in an unprecedented manner in this family, took control of the situation.

"Sir, your wife is very ill and realizes it. She is scared of many things…of growing old, of a disease that may have control over her, and of death itself. Victoria, your mother is very ill and needs you right now. So this is what is going to happen. Tomorrow you shall go back to New York with your Mother and Daddy. You will see to it that she gets the best of care that money can buy. Sir, you will attend to your business and wrap up lose ends there. For, if need be, you will need to be able to let the boys completely take over so that you can be with Inez full time to help care for her and spend every precious moment that you can with her. We will meet here as frequently as possible, and this includes the boys and Arthur and Verna. We will all see you through this, Inez, and we-the whole family-will be there to support you and take care of you. You mustn't worry about anything except getting well."

With these instructions given to each person in the room, Sam looked around and saw the approval and relief glowing from each face. William, Inez, and even Victoria realized in a sub-conscious way that they were all embarking on a journey which Sam knew more about. He was in charge, and they were content to have it that way.

Later that night while in bed, Sam asked Victoria, "Did I overstep my bounds earlier?"

"No, you sweet man. We all needed your strength and decisiveness. You acted perfectly." She sighed and continued, "You've had so much more experience than us with…"

She was hesitant to say the word 'death' and wanted to gloss it over and calm her own fears, so she said 'unhappiness' instead.

"I know." he said. "I know."

The next day it was as Sam had said. He said good-bye to three of the dearest people in his life. They were on their way to a city with some of the finest doctors in the world. Sam would have preferred to have them all near him so that he could help in decision making and to simply have his dear Virdie near him, but he knew that Inez needed her now more than he did.

Some of Victoria's last concerns were about her garden. He assured her that it would be well taken care of. He would see to that and he knew he could count on his parents to help. That's what family was for, he assured her.

The reunion when he arrived at Sunbury was difficult at first. Arthur and Verna took the news well, but wanted to leave immediately for New York. Sam calmed them by saying they had no idea what they were up against at this time and that in the future Inez and William may need them more than they did currently. They agreed that this was sound advice.

Then Sam went to see his own parents. They, of course, were very willing to help with Victoria's garden. Ann would see to it that it didn't suffer any, even if her own went by the wayside. Then they talked about life and death. They reminisced about the babies they had buried and about aunts and uncles from the past. The atmosphere was so much different here than at the mansion. Sam saw a stark difference between the accepting reality of poor, common people and the hopefulness of religious people with money to spend on doctors. It became a little confusing to know what to think, but he sensed that everyone depended on him for support and advice. He prayed he would be up to the challenge then walked back to his own home, quiet and dark without Virdie there.

The doctors were confounded. The first who checked her said he felt nothing was wrong except approaching old age. A second was consulted who declared her heart and lungs in fine shape and suggested she simply slow down some of her activities saying that she had "too many irons in the fire." The third felt her affliction had something to do with the brain, but straightforwardly commented that not enough research had been done yet to know what for sure. The Brittanhaur's visited doctors during the week when they could and came down to Cape Charles on weekends. Arthur and Verna slipped across the bay practically every other weekend. Sam was able to go at least once a month and sometimes twice. He assured Virdie that her garden was fine, and as proof he would take the latest and freshest produce. The entire family was impressed with the grand vegetables and the way that Victoria fixed them into appetizing dishes when they were together.

Alone in bed one Saturday evening, Sam asked his wife, "Seriously, how is your mother?"

"She's no better and I fear she is getting worse. She openly complains of the head aches now and frequently has to lie down to rest. The doctors are giving her no relief. In fact, they want to just prescribe morphine for pain and let it go at that."

Sam seemed shock. "Is the pain that bad?"

"Yes," Victoria replied. "It is at that point. But so far Mother has refused that."

"What do you do to help her relieve the pain?"

"I help give her a relaxing bath. I turn the lights down low. I rub her back or temples. I bring her tea." Her voice sounded strained and tired. "Sometimes when she can't sleep at night we just sit up and talk."

Sam mused more to himself than speaking to Virdie, but he said, "No, that won't do. I wonder…" Then, realizing his wife was giving him a puzzled look, he added, "Tomorrow you mustn't leave early. I've got to go back to the plantation early in the morning but I will be back before nightfall. Promise me you won't leave before I get back."

He sounded so insistent on some unknown errand that she said, "Of course, I promise." Then they fell into a restless sleep.

Sam was afraid what the others would think of his "home made recipes," but he gathered what herbs he needed, checked with his mother, and packed his supplies for the return trip to Cape Charles. It was a difficult day of hurrying and anxiety for him, but true to her promise, Victoria had insisted that the family not leave until Monday morning. By now her father reported in to the office only when absolutely necessary, so her brothers knew to manage everything when he was not around. They, for their part, felt as helpless as the rest concerning their mother's failing condition.

Sam practically ran up to the house and threw open the door, calling for Inez.

"Great! You're still here." He panted as he flew into the kitchen and pulled out some pans and lit a gas burner. "I need about a half hour to cook something up for you. Have you eaten? Good, because this isn't good on an empty stomach."

Sam mixed and concocted an unknown brew that Inez jokingly said smelled like a distillery. Sensing she was in a playful mood, which was rare these days, he replied, "And tell me, madam, how many distilleries have you visited lately?"

Inez laughed as she only could with Sam. Watching him intently, she perched on a kitchen chair and drew strength just from his presence. William and Victoria took the opportunity to spend a few moments without Inez. The moments not caring for her were far between, so they took this time to walk outside for a little and talk between the two of them about things other than their darling wife and mother.

When they returned home, they heard laughter ringing from the kitchen.

"You've made her drunk!" William stormed as he smelled the potion and saw his wife sitting lop-sided and giggling like a school girl.

"How dare you say such a thing to a kind boy who has made an old lady feel good for a little while!" Inez retorted quickly, much like her old self.

"What was that brew?" William turned his attention to Sam.

"Just some herbal tea with a secret family recipe," Sam laughed. "She needed a little relief and I guarantee it is non-addictive. She won't have a head ache for a few hours and she should sleep well tonight."

William and Sam discussed the smelly concoction. William at first was just curious to its contents, then when he was convinced there was nothing narcotic or alcoholic, he was curious as to how Sam knew of this and why others did not.

"As I said, it's an old family recipe. We usually use it for mothers giving birth, but I knew it was a powerful pain killer. We also used it when Walter had his gun accident. We hadn't had need of it for years and I had practically forgotten about it," Sam explained.

William's last question about the "wonder drug" caught Sam off guard and made him take William out to the hallway before he would answer. "Sir, there's a limited supply. I don't even know what some of these plants are that go into it. As far as I know, they're just weeds that grow around the plantation. But I do know that it won't last forever. I use the leaves. They have to be fresh. Once the plant withers and dries, they lose their value. I'm sorry, but after first frost there won't be any more."

William's countenance was so drawn that he looked like a man twice his age. "Can we take it to somewhere? Have it analyzed?" He knew he was groping for any help he could get for his wife, but he also knew the answer before he even asked.

With Sam's sad shake of his head, William sighed and said, "Then let her enjoy herself while she can. Thank you for what you have done. I'm sorry for being short with you earlier."

Like many times before, they patted each other on the shoulders and went to join the women in the kitchen, who were laughing over some shared joke.

By October the plant had withered and died. Inez was still trying various doctors, who prescribed everything from cool air in the north to humid air in the south. One suggested mineral springs in West Virginia while another claimed that hot water would only make her worse.

In the meantime, Victoria had visited a doctor also. Her ailment, though, was one that would bring much joy to the family when she finally told them. She was pregnant.

She wanted to tell Sam first, and when she did he stuttered and stammered, "What? How?"

She laughed and told him that apparently he knew how because she was.

"I mean, with you being gone so much and all," he said in a still puzzled voice.

"Well, it's not like we've been celibate the past few months. Every other week or so at Cape Charles..." she tried to explain in practical terms, but having regained his senses, Sam gently picked her up, swung her around and hugged her close to him.

"Oh, Virdie!" he exclaimed, "I am so happy I could nearly burst." With that he put his head near Victoria's tummy that showed no bulge yet and started speaking gently. "Hello, little one. I'm your Daddy. Oh, precious child, I love you so much."

His tenderness brought tears to her eyes, wonderful tears of joy to eyes that had shed a good deal of tears of sadness of late.

Then a reality of a different sort caught up with them.

"Have you told anyone yet?" Sam inquired.

"Of course not," she replied. "I wanted you to be the first to know, silly. Then we can tell them together."

They agreed to wait till the next day when Arthur and Verna were coming over for the weekend. Besides them, Edward and his family were coming to the seaside house. The family somehow sensed that each time they spent together may well be the last, as this would turn out to be.

While everyone squeezed into the parlor the next evening and chatted comfortably around a quiet fire in the fireplace, Victoria stood up, took Sam's hand, who stood beside her, and said, "Family, we have an announcement to make."

All eyes were upon them and Sam unconsciously blushed, feeling the dreaded redness creeping up his neck as when he was young.

"By next June there will be another member to this family." Victoria proclaimed.

There was a momentary hush while the significance of her words sank in. Then the room erupted with claps, cheers, and then everyone was on their feet, hugging Victoria and slapping Sam on the back. For them all, but particularly for Inez, the family felt whole. It was a great reunion and they each cherished the two days they had together.

All too soon Sam, Arthur and Verna needed to get back to the plantation.

"I'm sorry, but we are in the middle of harvest time," the men said, with real regret in their voices.

The rest of the family, including Victoria, headed north again toward New York City.

October went by with pleasant weather, but too soon November was upon them. With no more herbal teas as a pain killer, Inez began to spend entire days in bed. She moaned so much that sometimes William would sleep in a chair near her rather than in the bed. He didn't want to disturb her in any way. But Victoria knew from his sunken eyes and haggard look that he wasn't getting much sleep either.

"Daddy, please." she started one morning. "She's in such pain. Isn't it time for the morphine?"

"Oh, darling, I hate to…" he started, but then added, "Let's call the doctor in today."

In the early afternoon the family doctor who had attended them since the birth of all three children came to visit. He examined Inez then spoke to William and Victoria in the hall.

"She's very ill and at this point there isn't a thing I know to do for her." he started. "All we can do now is keep her as comfortable as possible and pray that the Lord will take her home soon."

This was an odd and conflicting idea in William's head as he hadn't been to church for many a year. But Victoria, having been under Arthur and Sam's care in the spiritual arena for some time, agreed and added, "We need to pray for mercy and grace."

At that point William vowed to go back to church as soon as this was over, but for now he would leave Inez' side only when absolutely necessary.

The family in Virginia was notified by phone of the latest turn in Inez' condition. It was decided that as many as possible would come to visit the last weekend of November. They might even plan an early Christmas, they said. William nixed that idea. He was afraid too much commotion in the house would only upset Inez more and make her feel that much more helpless. Her days were spent in holding his hand, reminiscing about better times whenever she was awake, and dozing frequently when the morphine set in.

As it turned out, the family's timing was perfect, but not in the way they had expected.

One morning when the day dawned bright and crisp, Inez woke cheerily and called for Victoria. "Please come sit with me for a little while," she said, "I'd like to take some tea and a roll with one of your famous jellies." That was the first food her mother had requested for so long, that Victoria's hopes rallied.

"Perhaps she's getting better," she told her father as she went toward the kitchen. William had felt the need to attend to some business at the office that day but instantly changed his mind. He called the office instead and requested that both brothers drop what they were doing and come immediately to the home. They quickly did as he requested.

Victoria fixed the meal as requested and took it to her mother's room. There she sat next to her while she ate. Then she cleared the dishes. When she came back up from the kitchen, she was surprised to see her Dad and both brothers there.

"What's going on?" she asked, alarmed.

"She doesn't have much longer, dear." William said, resignedly.

"That's not true! She's better today!" Victoria cried.

"Victoria, do you remember when Grandfather Brittanhaur was ill? Do you remember what happened the day before he died?" William was doing his best to bring her to an acceptance of reality in a gentle manner.

"I was too young," she retorted. "I don't know."

"Yes, you do, because we've told you the story numerous times." he said gently. "Grandfather had never heard you speak. The morning of the day he died he commented, 'Listen to that child babble. I've never heard her go on like that before.' You know they say that the senses all sharpen right before death. Dear, your mother is there. Let's just all be with her today…for one last time."

With a sigh that could break hearts at a lesser time, Victoria agreed.

They entered the bedroom with as cheery of faces as they could muster, saying, "Look, dear, the boys have come over to spend the day with us."

The day was spent holding Inez' hand and seeing to her needs. They talked about many lovely memories from days when the children were young. Inez commented more than once about the birds chirping outside her window. She asked to look out the window, so they helped her to sit in a comfortable chair.

"Look at all the squirrels playing," she commented. "I've never noticed so many in the yard before."

The little comments like that nearly made Victoria cry. She had to fight back tears as the chit-chat continued. She wondered why they were only talking about common, mundane things like birds and squirrels. Didn't her mother have any last pearls of wisdom to share with them? Didn't she have some proverbial blessing to pronounce upon her children like Jacob did for Isaac and Esau?

"Mother, please..." she started once, but her father quickly interrupted her.

"Aren't we all having a lovely day together, Inez? The sky is blue; the weather is perfect; it's a beautiful day."

"Yes," she agreed, "I feel so much better today. I feel calm and at peace."

That was all that needed to be said for William. He wanted her to be happy and to not be hurting for a change. It was merciful, he thought.

But Victoria still needed something more, and her mother seemed to sense that.

"You boys have always been a source of great pride for me," she began. "the way you have continued the family business and you, Edward, with starting a family of your own now. I am very proud of both of you."

She paused for a moment while collecting her thoughts. "As for you, Victoria, I don't mind admitting that you gave me many restless nights in earlier years. You and your obsession with a certain young man from Virginia." There her mother smiled sweetly, and continued. "But, my dear, I must admit that you were right. Sam is a perfect gentleman. In fact, he conducts himself better than many of the high society brats of your age who have contented themselves to live off their father's money. They never work. They drink and carouse too much. It is shameful!"

At this her mother had to stop to catch her breath. Anyone could tell it was a topic she felt strongly about and the heat of passion had nearly exhausted her. But she rallied and continued, "You chose wisely. Sam is a good man. He loves you and will always take care of you...and your child. Thank you for letting me know that you're expecting. It helps to know that as one life ends another begins."

There was a long silence in the room. Victoria held her mother's hands while the quiet tears streamed down her cheeks. The blessing was spoken. Plus, everyone in the room now knew that Inez knew she was at the end. She was calm. She had her family around her. She knew she had a good life. The end was near and she was ready.

"Please, now my loved ones, you have been so good to spend all day with me..."

The others interrupted her in protest, but she continued, "But right now I am very tired. Please leave me with just your father for a little while."

The children had no choice but to do as she wished. So each one in turn leaned over her, kissed her on the cheek, squeezed her hand, and said something like, "Yes, rest mother. We'll be right outside if you need us."

She smiled as they went out. "We raised fine children, didn't we, William?"

"Yes, my dear, fine children. They are very much like you, you know," his words coming out in a whisper as he sat beside her, holding her hand and smoothing her hair back with the other.

Inez took his hand and held it to her cheek then kissed it. "Don't be afraid. I…must….rest…now." The words came with longer pauses between each. Her eyes closed and her breathing became slower.

William sat there alone with his beloved bride for nearly two hours. He thought of the times when they didn't seem to be walking down the same road together. He thought of the times when he was too busy to attend to the needs of his family. He felt a lot of guilt and sorrow. Then she stirred.

"You were the perfect husband for me, and such a good father. Thank you." With that, she smiled, sighed, and went back to sleep.

To William, it was as if she had been reading his mind. Then he decided to let go of the regrets and wishes for what could have been. He made a conscious decision to preserve her memory as a happy one. She had been a good mother and a good wife. That was all he needed.

Within half an hour she stirred again, coughed, made a sort of gurgling sound, and then her whole body went limp. That was it. She had passed from one world to another as peacefully as could be expected. William sat there for another five minutes, sharing his last thoughts with her. Then he quietly got up and went to the door. The children were in the parlor downstairs. Victoria was dozing and the boys were talking quietly in front of the fireplace.

"It's done," he said softly.

Victoria awoke and looked at him. "Mother?"

"She's gone. She went quietly and peacefully, just as she wanted. She didn't want the three of you there to see that. She and I spent the last few moments together quietly, just as she wished. You may go see her now."

The children went upstairs, almost tip-toeing. They went into the room, paused in front of her bed, then each one did as they had before. They kissed her on the cheek, squeezed her hand, and said "Good-bye, mother."

Victoria made a special mental image of her mother's head resting on a pillow with a pillowcase that said "Hers."

The family from Virginia arrived two days later, as scheduled. They knew, though, that they were coming for a funeral because William had called them immediately after calling the doctor while the children were in the bedroom with her alone for one last time. All the arrangements were made. The funeral, which could have been a great social event, was a quiet, family oriented affair. After the burial, the family all came back to the house, where a large meal had been set up by the household servants. The family sat and ate quietly, with very little talking going on.

The next day, a cold November morning, dawned bright and crisp. The Virginia family prepared to meet their train heading south. Victoria seemed torn. Finally she went to her father and said, "Oh, Daddy, it hurts me to leave you. You will be so lonely now in this big old house. Now you need me more than ever."

But he stopped her with a finger to her lips. He turned his eyes toward Sam, who was standing there with suitcases in his hands. "No, darling, you have done your duty to your mother. I have things I must do here for a while. Your place is not with me. It is with your husband and in your own home. I will miss you, but you must go now."

Sam set down the bags and shook William's hand. So many unspoken words had passed between them in this way so many times before.

"Take care of my baby....no, my babies." William grinned as he corrected himself and patted Victoria's tummy which was just beginning to bulge a little.

"You know I will, sir. You know I will." Sam smiled and nodded in confirmation. Then they were gone.

William wasn't sure how to spend Christmas that year. He wanted to be with Victoria, but there was no room in their home on the plantation. He could have stayed with his brother Arthur at Sunbury, but he wasn't sure he wanted to be in a huge house full of Christmas cheer. So, he spent the day at Edward and Susan's house and doted on little Evelyn, who adored her grandfather. Then he slipped away to Cape Charles for a few days by himself. No one came to visit as no one knew he was there. He wanted it that way. He felt that by himself sometimes he could hold the memory of his wife more sacred and closer to his heart. Yes, he was still grieving, he admitted to himself. Even though she could be a hard-nosed, straight-laced busy body, he had loved her. And that was that. But after a few days' reflection, he also realized he had a lot to be thankful for. The Christmas Eve sermon had reminded him of that. True to his word, he had started to go back to church and he realized that he was blessed with a successful business, healthy and happy children, grandchildren, and his own health. Life was good and he would endeavor to enjoy it.

CHAPTER 9

▼

THE SPRING

January and February found the family spending a lot of time together. This was the time of year when things were slow at the plantation, so Arthur and Verna and Sam and Victoria took advantage of it to slip away to Cape Charles. William was always there, having found a new pleasure in cooking and caring for himself. He had not reduced the household staff any at the home in New York, although he knew he needed to soon. Money wasn't a concern for him, so neither was running or maintaining a household.

The times together were quiet and happy. Arthur summed it up best when he said, "We have seen many things in our lifetimes, William. Each day brings something new. We just have to be aware of what it is and appreciate it."

Arthur and Verna shared in William's anticipation of Victoria and Sam's baby, but they were also anticipating more of their own. Elizabeth was pregnant again and due in August. Sarah was engaged to be married to James from Obici in late June. They had planned the wedding to not interfere with the arrival of Victoria and Sam's baby. Mary and Margaret were both being courted by young gentlemen from the Norfolk area, and Verna and Arthur expected engagement announcements from them any time.

As for William's family, Edward and Susan professed to be trying to have another child, but none was forth coming yet. Paul appeared at some social events, but he seemed fairly content to help Edward with the business and spend quiet weekends by himself.

All in all, the Brittanhaur brothers felt content with life.

On the plantation, the winter had been a mild one. Sam had made sure that all the farm machinery was in good repair and ready for spring planting. He had cleared more land between his house and his parents, using the cut wood for heating and spending the mild winter days burning brush and cutting weeds and trees. Arthur was always pleased with the way Sam continued to work. He was always improving the barns, sheds, and land. Even though they weren't his, he always did his best. William appreciated that and made sure little treats found their way to Sam and Victoria's house.

By March Sam was anxious to get into the fields. William advised waiting a while longer and it turned out to be a good thing that they did. A harsh blizzard blew in that closed everything down for miles around. All roads were blocked, and everybody with any sense stayed indoors.

Sam and Victoria had seen the storm coming on the horizon. They had plenty of wood, food, and books to read. So they spent two days snowed in to their little home. Sam didn't seem as restless as the other times when he couldn't be outdoors because he had brought some fine oak into the house. He spent many hours in front of the fire, carving, sanding, and finishing a little cradle. When it was finished, he presented it to Victoria. She was amazed at the excellent handiwork. Not only was the wood silky to the touch, Sam had carved a beautiful bird into the headboard. It was perfect. No words could tell him how much she adored this simple gift that had taken so much time. She knew how much love he had poured into it and how much he was anticipating being a father. He talked to the child now growing and kicking in her tummy often. It even seemed that the child responded when he talked to her. Victoria felt in her heart that the child was a girl, although she didn't say anything about it to Sam. He claimed he would be happy with either a boy or a girl, but she felt that he really wanted a boy to follow him around and teach things to.

Others in the family were also busy preparing things for the baby's arrival. Ann was sewing fine dresses, delicately edged with tatting that she had made herself. Javan was also working with wood, preparing a rocking horse for the child. Arthur and Verna had been shopping in Suffolk on one of their trips to Cape Charles and had bought leather shoes. Victoria had chuckled at that gift as she knew it was extravagant and unnecessary, but a fond token of the feelings they all shared for each other. William, also, doted on the child but in a different way. He bought the mother treats. He made sure that every time they got together he had some special delicacy for Victoria. He always asked, "Are you eating properly, my dear?"

To this she would smile and answer "Yes, Daddy." and then indulge herself in the treat he had brought her.

April brought plenty of sunshine and warmth. Sam was out in the fields, happy as a lark. It is true that he came and checked in on Victoria more often than he used to. She was more often at home. Ann helped her plant her garden, assuring her that it would be taken care of when the baby came. Victoria had no doubt about that, as her garden had been well taken care of last fall when she had spent time with her mother.

Victoria could often be found in the afternoons rocking on the porch, some kind of stitching in her hand. Sometimes she would set the cloth down, watch the birds and squirrels and think about her mother. She thought it would have brought her much sadness to think that her own mother wasn't going to get to see her grandchild, but it didn't. Victoria thought about the rightness of things, the passing of the seasons one after the other in good time. She thought about nature and God. At times like these, she amazed herself at how content she felt. Those days of social events in New York were long gone. She knew her hands were rougher than those of women her age she had grown up with. But she also prided herself on how many things she could do for herself. She could keep a clean house. She could cook, sew, and garden. She could can and make preserves. She knew in her heart that she had been made for this kind of simple life. Compared to the night life of the city, many thought her life dull, but she loved it. She felt at peace, at home, and totally in love and loved. She couldn't imagine life ever being any different than it was this very day.

Sam came up the path and saw her day-dreaming.

"A penny for your thoughts," he said quietly so that he wouldn't startle her.

"Oh, my!" she jumped. "You must think I'm so lazy! You caught me day-dreaming here on this beautiful day when I should be..."

"What? What should you be doing?" he laughed as he came up and kissed her gently on the cheek. "You should be doing exactly what you are doing. Resting. Letting our child grow strong and healthy. Letting yourself get strong and healthy for the delivery."

A cloud seemed to come across Victoria's face.

"Sam? Have you ever thought that I might..." she didn't have the nerve to finish the question. It was too horrid a thought.

"No." Sam said confidently. "You're small, but you are healthy and happy and I'm sure everything will go fine."

This made her laugh and the cloud passed by. "I'm small? Look at the size of me! I can't fit through the door sideways!"

"You're not supposed to fit through the door sideways, you silly thing." Then they both erupted into laughter and she felt the baby kicking strongly. "Oh, stop!" she cried, "It hurts!" but they continued to laugh anyway.

As the calendar turned a new page to May, the family came to visit Victoria more often and she went out less often. The weather, to her, seemed unbearably warm. She felt huge, awkward, and very ready to have this baby.

One afternoon as she sat on the front porch with Ann, she asked her mother-in-law about her deliveries.

"Well, darlin', each one was different. I reckon some women are just made for birthing babies and others are meant for other things."

An uneasy quiet settled between them for a brief moment. Ann could tell that Victoria was nervous about the up-coming delivery, so she said, "You'll do fine. I'll be here. Your Aunt Verna will be here. And who knows who else will be here."

Vicky smiled at her mother-in-law fondly and took her hand. "You know, I'd rather have just you and Sam here than anyone else. With the two of you by my side, I know I can do anything."

The two women held hands for a moment and smiled lovingly at each other. Some things are better left unsaid.

Several nights later Sam awoke from a terrible dream with sweat dripping off his face. He sat up in bed, wiped the sweat thinking "It's not that hot yet." then remembered the details of his dream. He didn't want to risk waking Virdie as she was finding it increasingly difficult to get comfortable and get to sleep within the last week, so he quietly eased himself back into the bed and lay there with his eyes closed, praying more fervently than he had ever prayed before.

Virdie, who normally would have noticed the dark circles under her husband's eyes and his slowness of movement the next morning, didn't notice at all. She was preoccupied with lifting her protruding stomach out of bed and getting herself dressed in something that would fit around her.

"Oh, Sam? How much longer? I feel so..." and she started to cry.

"Please, dear, today you must not over-exert yourself. Your emotions are running rampant and your body is working over-time to feed this growing child.

Please, today just rest." he begged, with visions from his dream popping into his head without invitation.

"I fear there isn't anything else I can do," she admitted, and sat down in the rocker.

"Can you pack your own lunch? I just don't seem to have the strength to do it right now."

"Yes, don't you worry about me. I'll be fine and I'll be in to check on you as often as I can," he promised as he walked out the front door.

Sam's first chore of the morning, though, was not to water the horses or work in the field. His first stop took him directly to Sunbury. He found Arthur up and about, but all the womenfolk still in bed.

"Sir?" he called in the open front door through the screen.

"Sam, my boy. Come in, come in. How are you this fine morning?"

"To tell you the truth sir, I'm starting to not sleep so well and Victoria is even worse."

"Yes, yes," he said calmly and with a far away look in his eyes. "I remember the nights just before Verna delivered Elizabeth. The first is the worst, my boy, because of the unknown. After that, it's a breeze and they worry about it less."

"Yes, well, I was wondering if perhaps your wife or girls could go visit with Vicky today, if it's not too much trouble. She seems so uncomfortable and out of sorts. I'm afraid I'm not much comfort to her."

"Well, I know you are a comfort to her, but I will send the girls along just the same. She really shouldn't be alone for too long at a time like this, anyhow. Please feel free to check on her anytime you feel you need to. You know the fields will still be there when you get back."

Arthur Brittanhaur smiled with a kind, understanding smile and Sam knew that he had done the right thing, even though the previous night's dream still haunted him.

About mid-morning Ann stopped by to work in Vicky's garden for a while. She wanted to do it before it got too hot. Vicky would have preferred for her mother-in-law to just sit and talk to her for a while, but she knew the work needed to be done, too. At this point, she was simply too big to bend over and pull weeds or climb a tree to pick cherries, no matter how much she wanted to.

After the work was done, Ann visited for a while and made sure that Victoria had some lunch. Then she went on home, saying that she needed to feed Javan. "Poor man never learned to fend for himself much. Guess I spoiled him by waiting on him hand and foot, but you know I love him so. The old coot."

Victoria just smiled as she watched the older lady lumber back down the pathway toward her house. She hoped that she would be as spry physically and mentally when she was that age.

Not long after that, Mary and Margaret came for a call, carrying a freshly baked cherry pie.

"My, does that ever smell good!" Victoria exclaimed. "Can I have a piece now?"

"Well, it was supposed to be for supper, but why not? You two can't eat a whole pie for supper now, can you?" And the girls all laughed, noticing that Vicky's piece was bigger than normal. But then, she was eating for two!

The girls stayed for over an hour just talking about the local gossip and the beaus they were currently seeing. They discussed Sarah's future wedding and what a social event that would be. It seemed that Arthur and Verna spared no expense when it came to their girls, and their weddings were some of the greatest social events of the area.

"I sure do hope to be able to dance a waltz or two by then," Victoria sighed.

"You mustn't push yourself too much," Mary warned. "Remember that it took Elizabeth a month or more to recover from her delivery of little Art. Mama says that you can hurry it up then, but it just takes longer in the long run."

Margaret added her two cents' worth. "Personally, if I had people waiting on me and taking care of everything for me, I wouldn't be inclined to get out of bed at all."

The girls all laughed good-naturedly because they knew that was close to the truth. Sarah could be lazy at times, but as the baby of the family Margaret had her fair share of chores done for her whenever she over-slept or feigned a head ache.

The girls left and it wasn't too long before William appeared, cresting the small knoll that blocked the view of Sunbury from Sam and Vicky's house.

"Daddy!" Victoria cried as she tried to get up and go toward him.

"Stay there, darling, I'm coming!" he called.

He picked up his pace and shortly arrived at his daughter's side.

"Daddy, I'm so glad to see you! But look at me, oh my!"

Victoria's father reassured her that she was the most beautiful thing on the face of the earth. He sat beside her for an hour, telling her about his trip from Cape Charles, having arrived at about noon.

"How long can you stay?" Victoria asked.

"As long as I wish. Your brothers have complete control over the business. The house in New York is well taken care of. The extra help that I didn't need there I moved down to Cape Charles. Odd how they didn't mind going, either. 'To stay employed for you,' they told me, 'We'd go to Timbuktu.' Well, I told them I had no intention of going to Timbuktu or any other exotic place. But Cape Charles looks and feels more like home all the time now. I'm thinking of letting Edward and Susan just have the house in New York. What do you think?"

They discussed the financial aspects of that for a while and Vicky was truly glad to have her mind occupied with something other than weddings, girl talk, and babies. She felt 100% better by the time her father announced that he needed to get back to the mansion.

She agreed reluctantly, but only after her father promised to come see her on the morrow.

It wasn't too long after that that Sam arrived home from the fields. He cleaned up some, then prepared a meal for the two of them.

"Look what I have for supper!" Vicky said proudly and produced the cherry pie with a rather large piece missing.

"Well, young lady!" he teased. "That is the most unusual looking style of pie I have ever seen. Truly unique-just like you."

She giggled, then he asked, "Really, now, how did you do it?"

She admitted that the girls had brought it earlier and she couldn't resist having "just a small piece." They laughed and enjoyed a good humored meal together. Sam told her everything about this year's crops and how the livestock were doing. She told him all the gossip from town and about her father's news about the house.

"That's a fine idea, I think," Sam commented. "They will need a bigger house soon, and he doesn't need it. Best to keep it in the family."

Victoria was glad that there was no jealousy between herself and her brothers. Her father had always treated them individually, but as close to equally as he could. She prayed that she would be as good a parent as he.

One of the conversations between Verna and Victoria the next day included the fact that Victoria had not been sick at all during the first three months of her pregnancy. She compared herself to her sister-in-law, Susan, who had been terribly ill, but had an easy delivery. She asked her aunt if she thought this would be a difficult delivery because she had such an easy time of it at the beginning.

Verna commented, "Well, honey, you just never know. The Lord knew that you didn't need to be sick while caring for your mother, so I figure He just took that illness away. The rest is up to Him, too. Just trust that He knows what He's doing."

Victoria was glad to hear Verna's viewpoint. It was always filled with faith and had no room for human frailties or doubt. She presented her views gently without any admonition for lack of faith, and when she did Victoria felt comforted.

June arrived and the next two days and nights followed much the same pattern. Neither Sam nor Victoria slept well, but did their best not to wake the other. Sam spent his days working on the plantation, as usual. Victoria spent her days feeling more and more tired, grateful for the company that came to occupy her mind, but wishing for more rest even though she wasn't doing anything but sitting.

Bright and early on the morning of June 3, Victoria was up and out of bed before Sam. She had the coffee on the stove to brew and had a broom in her hand when he came out of the bedroom and looked at her, puzzled.

"Good morning, lazy bones," she started as she went over and gave him a kiss. Your lunch is packed. Breakfast is on the stove. The coffee is ready. The sun is up, and it is going to be a glorious day!"

Her enthusiasm and energy made him wonder if he was in the right house.

"Virdie? Are you OK?" he questioned.

"Couldn't be better," she responded. "I finally feel so good. I slept well last night and I'm tired of just sitting around feeling sorry for myself. It's time to do something, so get out of here and leave me to do those things that women do best."

He nodded, still stunned, and did as she said. But today, rather than head straight for Sunbury and the barns, he headed in the opposite direction toward his parent's house.

Once he got there, he told his mother about the drastic change in Victoria.

"She's nesting," his Mom replied, as if that would explain everything.

Sam, still with a puzzled look on his face, asked if she would go by early to see Vicky.

"Sam, honey, you don't get it, do you? Vicky has extra energy today because today is the day the baby will come. She is like a mother bird, preparing her nest for her baby. Now get yourself on up to the big house and tell them up there to be on stand-by. I'm setting off right now for your place. You'd better plan to come back around lunch just to see what's happening."

Sam was grateful that his mother seemed knowledgeable and confident of the day's events. The nightmares of recent nights still afflicted him. He envisioned Vicky doing too much, tiring herself out, and not having the strength for delivering the baby. His concern was so great that he took a short cut across the fields to get to Sunbury quicker.

Once there, he shared his news. He made them promise not to alarm Vicky by all rushing down there at once. But, on the other hand, he didn't want her working herself to death. So he explained that his mother was on her way and left other decisions up to the Brittanhaurs. William, of course, wanted to head down immediately. The others agreed that if anyone could get Victoria to sit down and rest, it would be he. The ladies would make last minute preparations, fix a good hot meal, then be down later.

Victoria found everyone converging on her house at once. She dismayed, "Please, I'm not ready for company yet. My hair is a mess and the house needs a good dusting. Oh, my, and look at these windows. They are filthy. I'm so sorry. Please, couldn't you come back later?"

Ann laughed and said, "Honey, you go sit on that porch and talk with your Daddy. I'll dust and wash those windows. Now don't you fret about a thing."

Vicky started to protest, but Ann took her gently but firmly by the arm and directed her to the porch.

"She's so good to me, you know," she started, then stopped to cry. "Oh, Daddy, she's such a good mother, but she's so different from Mother. I miss her, you know, but I'm really glad to have Ann here with me right now."

"Yes, honey. I know. Your mother was a special woman. She was brought up to be a certain kind of lady, and she was the best one she could be. Ann, on the other hand, is a different kind of lady, but a lady none the less. She is a good one to have around on a day like today."

"A day like today? What kind of day is today, Daddy?" asked Victoria.

"Well, honey, today is the day your baby will be born."

"What?" Victoria practically screeched. "Does everybody know that but me?"

William chuckled, took her hand and patted it, and said, "Yes, dear. We all knew about 'nesting' but you. That's why you mustn't work right now. All that extra energy is for labor. You'll start any time now. So in the meantime, sit with me here and be ready for when the time comes."

"I should be angry at all you conspirators, but I'm so glad to have you all here!" then she laughed, too. "Does Sam know?"

"Of course. He didn't know what 'nesting' was, but his description of your early morning activities today tipped us all off. He went to his mother first, then to Sunbury. Everything is being prepared, even as we speak."

Victoria looked surprised, "You all are really too much. I feel so lazy and helpless!"

"Honey, don't. You have the most important job of all. That's why it's called 'labor.'"

They smiled at each other and Ann appeared in the doorway. "What other jobs need to be done today, honey?"

"None, thank you, Ann. Thank you for humoring me. Daddy has explained what's going on and I promise to settle down now and attend to the business at hand." She smiled. "I do think, though, that I would like some tea, but first I need to visit the little building out back."

She rose to get up and as she did, fluid trickled down her legs. Mortified to think that she had just wet herself, Victoria blushed and began to apologize.

"Honey, your water just broke," Ann said. "Go to the bathroom now and when you get back from there, it's straight to bed for you."

Victoria went around the corner and William and Ann discussed the matter. They both knew this could take a long time, so they both decided to stay. William said others would be down around lunch time. He would take a break then and try to rest a little as it might be a long night.

"What about you? Will you be alright?" he asked Ann.

"Yes, sir. I'll be just fine. This poor little thing doesn't know what's coming and with her Mama not being here and all, I reckon I'll just stay with her and keep her going."

"I'm glad you're here, Ann. I really am. Thank you for all you're doing for my daughter."

"She's my daughter, too, you know." Ann chastised, but in a loving way.

The two of them grinned at each other, knowing that a young lady they both adored and loved would have a rough day and needed them both, but in different ways.

Victoria came back and was put to bed. Ann started boiling water and William sat by her bed and held her hand. Shortly thereafter the labor pains began. At first they were mild. Victoria commented about having a back ache.

"That's just part of the deal," William told her. "Your mother complained a lot of back aches during labor with you."

"Tell me more, Daddy. Tell me what each one of us was like." she begged.

As William started with Edward, the oldest, and tried to remember every detail, Victoria would squeeze his hand every so often. That was when the pains set in. William tried not to, but he checked his watch each time. Ten minutes. That's good, he thought to himself. As he told her about her mother's pregnancies, he realized that he had never been in the room at the actual time of birth.

Although many babies were born at home, as were all three of his, Inez' mother had insisted that a doctor attend each birth. He was "allowed" to wait downstairs in the parlor. He recalled pacing, almost running as she screamed in pain. He tried to omit that part, but realized that Victoria needed to know it was acceptable to be loud-to scream and yell if that helped any. So he spared her no details.

Ann, for her part, tinkered with things outside the bedroom. Every now and then she would peak her head in then scamper back out. She seemed to be very busy, but Victoria couldn't imagine with what. The house was clean. The garden was tidy. What more was there to do?

Around noon the women from Sunbury arrived. They brought a clear soup that was similar to chicken noodle. Victoria managed to eat some. By now her contractions were eight minutes apart and it wasn't long after eating that they became six minutes apart. Everything seemed to be progressing nicely.

Sam had stopped by at lunch time, checked on his wife and was summarily informed that his presence was not needed yet. He was to go back to work and come back in four hours.

Verna reassured him, "These things take time. There's no sense having you under foot here when you don't need to be. We'll be sure you're here when all the action takes place."

Now it was Verna's turn to sit and hold Victoria's hand. Again, stories of pregnancies and deliveries abounded. Verna, like William, did not leave out the details, and being a mother, she had a slightly different perspective on it.

"Yes, honey," she soothed, "it will hurt for a while. But I guarantee that you will soon forget all that in the joy of holding that precious little child."

Ann had gone home to feed Javan and to take a little nap. The experienced ladies all knew it could be a long night, but at this point they agreed that there seemed to be no problems and all was progressing well.

By five o'clock when Sam returned, Victoria's contractions were three minutes apart.

"How much longer?" Sam wailed, tired of being sent out of the house again.

"Another three hours, I'd guess," said Verna, and Ann agreed.

At sunset Sam had done everything he could think to do. He had watered, brushed, and fed every animal. He had oiled saddles and tack. He had watered his parent's garden and their own. He had eaten supper and paced the floor.

"Enough!" he cried. "I want to be with her now!"

He marched into the bedroom, unprepared for what he saw. Victoria lay on the bed, soaked in sweat. Her usually fine hair was plastered to her head. Her skin looked mottled from crying. She was panting and doing her best not to scream.

Sam's look of shock made her try to smile and say something to him, but another contraction overtook her. She gritted her teeth, moaned, then wailed uncontrollably.

"Oh, Virdie, I'm sorry. I'm so sorry. What do you want me to do?" he cried in such a pitiful voice that the mothers in the room considered sending him out again immediately, but Victoria intervened.

"Please, let him stay," she panted, and then she took his hand and squeezed with all her might.

Sam winced. "For such a little thing, you sure do have a grip," he tried to laugh, but it sounded strained. After that he sat at her side and just cooed, "I'm here for you. You squeeze as hard as you need to. Let me take the pain away. I'm here, darling."

After an hour of this, the mothers stepped outside the bedroom for a moment. William was in the living room area and looked up with anticipation. He was surprised to see the look of concern on the ladies' faces.

"What...what's the matter?" he nearly whispered.

"It's not getting any faster. She should have delivered by now." Verna told him with a very serious look on her face.

Ann added, "I've seen this before. I think the baby is breech. That means it wants to come out feet first instead of head first as it should."

She saw his look of concern so continued, "It can be done, but not usually for a first baby. It's harder. We need help now."

"William, please be so kind as to run up to the house and tell Arthur to go fetch the doctor," Verna said. "And please tell him to be quick."

He was on his way without a word. The women went back into the room. Ann had prepared her herbal tea, but Victoria was beyond the point of being able to eat or drink anything. The pain would just have to come, as would that baby.

Nearly an hour later the doctor arrived. He did a quick examination of his patient, then stepped out of the room again and motioned for the mothers to follow.

"Here's where we're at," he started. "The baby is breech, as you thought. It has already started down the birth canal, so it's too late to do a Caesarian. She is going to have to deliver it normally. It will be hard and there will be a lot of bleeding. She will tear on the inside. The baby will need to be very strong because this has gone on for nearly 12 hours. The baby is tired and the mother is tired. We've got to keep her going till it's delivered. After that, only the Lord knows."

The three looked at each other grimly. The mothers wondered each to themselves if the outcome would have been better had they called for the doctor earlier. But no, there was no sense in second guessing. It just wasn't that common to call in the doctor for everything.

"Let's go to work."

They re-entered the room. The doctor told Sam an abbreviated version of what he had just said to the ladies. His emphasis was that if he was in the way or couldn't stand the blood and screaming, he should leave now.

Sam said, "She and I are a team. We're in this together. I'm not leaving her side-now or ever!"

Privately, they were all glad. At this point Ann had a sinking feeling. This was so much like her grandchild that had died in birth. It was Charlie and Julia's second. The little boy was breech. Julia lived, although it was doubtful for a while because she had lost so much blood. But the poor baby took one breath and then didn't have the strength for another. She had been present at that birth, just as she had all her grandchildren. It was a fact she was proud of, but some of the memories were very painful.

Verna, for her part, was thinking of how easily she had delivered all four of her girls. But she had friends who had difficulties in delivery. She had heard the horror stories. At present it was all she could do to keep her composure and feign to help.

Just then the doctor instructed Victoria to push. She was leaning forward, gripping Sam's hand for all she was worth, gritting her teeth, and pushing. The blood began to pour forth. The ladies noticed that it wasn't just a trickle, not like the clear fluid of before. This was pure, red blood. They knew their jobs now. Keep it cleaned up as best as possible. The doctor would be busy later and he would need to see clearly what was going on.

They all heard noises in the other room. William, Arthur, Sarah, Mary, Margaret, and even old Javan were there. It was a room full of people in a small space. Arthur kept boiling water and finding clean rags. The girls mostly stood around horrified, so they were sent home to get more cloths. Javan kept the fire going in the fireplace and under the kettle.

Sam, for his part, felt helpless. Everyone seemed to have some important job to do but him. All he could do was sit and hold Victoria's hand. The sweat rolled down his face, too, but it wasn't from the heat. It was that awful cold sweat that comes from fear and has a smell all its own. He recognized it for such, but was unable to do anything about it.

After a half hour and what seemed like gallons of blood, the doctor crowed, "Good! We're getting somewhere now. I can see some little feet. Keep pushing. You're doing great! Pretty soon you'll hold this precious child."

Victoria pushed with all her strength. Sam noticed that the grip on his hand seemed less strong than before. He couldn't tell if he imagined it or it really was. "Keep going," he crooned. "She's almost here."

It was the first that Victoria had heard him say 'she' in reference to the baby. So he knew in his heart, too. That was a comfort. She smiled up at him but was too tired to say a word.

She pushed, and pushed and pushed some more. The doctor said he had hold of some feet around the ankle with his forceps. He was going to help now. Very carefully, so that he wouldn't deform or break the tiny feet and ankles, he began to apply pressure to help the baby come out. Victoria pushed, but the doctor could tell that she was near exhaustion. He wondered if she had it in her to do the last little bit herself. "Come on, now, just a little more."

She pushed with all her might, thinking in her mind that she had to do this just one more time. That's all. Just once more and she would be done. So she did.

The sound of tearing echoed through the room. It was so unexpected. Victoria screamed in abandon, not caring at that point what anyone else heard or thought. Sam grabbed her to him as best he could in his position. Both mothers dabbed at the blood that poured forth from her even stronger than before. The doctor, for his part, was busy with the baby. He held up a little girl for all to see. Just as he was about to swat her little behind, she let out one weak moan, shuddered, then turned blue.

"No you don't, you little thing." the doctor said, almost cursing. Then he began resuscitation on her. He cleaned out her mouth. He pumped her lungs. He blew air into her. He worked on the little body for nearly five minutes while everyone else seemed to freeze their gaze on him.

In reality, the mothers continued to wipe up blood. Sam and Victoria held each other. She panted and moaned. He whimpered in helplessness as he watched the horrible scene taking place in slow motion in front of him.

Finally, the doctor looked up. With tears in his eyes he sobbed, "I'm sorry. She was too tired out. I've tried everything I know to do. Now I've got to attend to this bleeding before…"

His words trailed away because the look on his face gave away the fact that the rest of his sentence was going to be "…it's too late."

Verna took the infant and handed her to Victoria. "Look, darling, she was a perfect little girl."

Victoria cradled the baby near her bosom and cried uncontrollably. Sam put his huge hand upon the little head where a shock of light colored hair was matted down. "Oh, my baby. Oh, my darling." he whispered, with the tears rolling down his cheeks.

Ann had slipped out of the room unnoticed to tell the others what was going on. When she slipped back in, she took the child, wrapped her in a clean cloth of the softest sort, kissed the little cheek, then passed her to Verna. Verna took another clean cloth, wiped the child's hands and arms clean, then kissed her other cheek. Everyone was crying uncontrollably at that point.

"Ladies, we are not done here. I need your help and you must do what I say immediately. This is crucial." The tone of the doctor's voice at that moment brought them all back to the fact that another emergency was looming.

"Take the baby to the other room and quickly return with more thread and rags. Sam, hold her down. This is going to hurt and she must not move. Victoria, I'm sorry, honey, but right now I've got to sew you up. It will hurt. Please focus on some picture or Sam's face and think about something else. You have got to hold still. Please."

By the time he finished with his commands, the mothers had returned. They were one on each side of Victoria, near her knees, helping to hold her down. The doctor wiped his eyes once, then said, "Ready? Here we go."

Sam risked one glance at what was going on at the foot of the bed and nearly passed out. He had to focus on Victoria's face, he knew. He had to help her. "I'm here" he crooned over and over because it was the only thing he could say.

Within a minute Victoria passed out. Her body went rigid. The doctor looked up and said, "Just make sure she's still breathing."

Sam leaned closer, feeling her breath on his cheek, but ever so gently.

Then something happened. Whether the doctor was trying to stitch too far in or he hit a nerve or what, no one will ever know, but Victoria came to with a start, screamed, shuddered, and passed out again. This time, her breathing stopped.

"Doc, I'm losing her. Help!" Sam yelled.

The doctor forgot his sewing and came up with his stethoscope to listen to her heart. It was weak. He tried resuscitating her. Air. Massage. Calling her name loudly. A slap on the face. Strong spirits under her nose. No. He was losing her, too.

"William! Get in here!" It was Verna who had presence of mind enough to call in her father.

"Help us! Call her."

William rushed to her side with Sam. The doctor was on the other side. William, with a rush of commanding force screamed, "Victoria! Don't you die on me!"

"Daddy, oh, Daddy." Her eyes flickered and tried to open. Then she focused wearily on Sam. "Sam, oh, Sam."

With that her eyes closed and her head rolled to the side. The doctor worked in silence for what seemed like an eternity, then he looked up. Tears were rolling down his cheeks as he quietly said, "I'm sorry."

Shock set in immediately. Everyone held still. Not daring to move. Not daring to breathe. Not daring to think that the unthinkable had happened.

When William had rushed into the room he had left the door open. By now Arthur, Javan, and the three girls were gathered around it.

The doctor wiped his eyes and face with his shirt sleeve, stood up, and said, "Take as long as you wish. Then I will finish up." With that, he walked out into the night.

There was a sliver of a moon in the sky. As he stood on the porch looking up, his heart pleaded, "Why, God?" but he knew the answer. He knew from experience that some things were bigger than he was. He knew that only God was the Divine Physician. He was only human. And so, as he began to notice the sweat chilling on his skin, he whispered to himself, "Into Thy hands I commend them both." He took a deep breath, sighed, and realized how tired he was. He sat down in the rocking chair there when he was joined by Javan.

"Thanks for trying, Doc. I know you did all you know how." And he patted the doctor's back. The two of them stayed on that porch for a few more minutes and they both noticed the night birds singing.

Quietly the three girls joined them. There were no words to be said, but none felt the power to leave the quiet little home.

"Life goes on." the doctor said to no one in particular.

"Tell that to Sam." It was Ann's voice. She, too, had quietly slipped out and stood beside her husband. "Go on home," she said to her husband. "I'll stay and help clean up."

"Yes, let's get it done," said the doctor.

So Javan headed for his little hut. Arthur took his three girls toward the mansion. They all realized that it wasn't the size of the house, the amount of money in the bank, or the number of acres you plowed that made any difference at that point. Family. Friends. Love. Happiness.

With William on one side and Sam on the other, the doctor and the mothers finished doing what needed to be done. The two men both sat there, staring blankly. Unable to say a word. Lost in their own thoughts. They shared only one thing: that both of them had lost the most precious woman in the world to them.

Finally, the doctor said, "If it's alright with you, we will leave the mother and the child in the bed with her for tonight. Tomorrow we'll make other arrangements."

With a nod, Sam approved. William stood up, leaned over his daughter, and kissed her forehead. Then he kissed the forehead of the baby. Sam did the same. The two men exited the room and quietly shut the door behind them.

"Sam?" William started tentatively. "Where will you sleep tonight? Do you want to come up to Sunbury with me? I'm sure…"

His voice trailed off.

"I won't." Sam said with no color to his voice.

"I know. Me either." The familiar hand was on his shoulder.

Sam began to sob and with that, so did William. Each needed the release. Each needed the comfort of the other. They hugged each other until the bad time passed.

Then Sam said with resolve, "I will stay here tonight. I will sleep here, in the chair. In case they need me."

"Yes." William whispered as Sam indicated the rocking chair near the fireplace. "Yes."

With that, he headed into the dark toward the mansion, knowing that Sam would sit up all night, and wishing that he could, too.

Arthur had made all the arrangements very early the next day. Victoria and the baby were laid in a beautiful wooden coffin in the large parlor at Sunbury. The family received guests that evening. The household servants had prepared and spread out many dishes that kept well in the early summer heat. Neighbors came and went. Elizabeth, with her husband and child, came for a little while but soon went home as she, too, was expecting, and the sight of the young mother and baby disturbed her greatly.

Sam sat in a straight-backed chair near the coffin all evening. He had on his suit that had been made for his first trip to Cape Charles. All luster seemed to be gone from him. Of course, he hadn't done any of the normal chores that day. He seemed to not even think about the animals that he enjoyed working with or the fields where the first sprouts were shooting out of the ground.

William was grieving, also, but his was different. He avoided the parlor. He spent his time outdoors as much as possible, but even that was painful. Every little thing seemed to remind him of Victoria. The trees. The fresh air. The birds. Especially the birds.

In the evening air he sat on the bench under the old magnolia tree where Sam and Victoria had sat several years before, holding hands and talking about life. He felt as if someone had torn his heart from his chest. He sat there, wanting to sob, wanting to hug his daughter to him and comfort her, wanting to die in her place.

"Lord, why?" he whispered.

Then Arthur appeared. He sat down by his brother and patted him on the shoulder. "I had a hard time finding you."

"Didn't really want to be found." William replied.

"I know." The two men sat in silence for a long time. It was dark. After a while, Arthur broke the silence, "What will you do after tomorrow?"

William must have been thinking a lot about that. His thoughts were hard to sort out. He knew he shouldn't make any decisions based on emotion, but it was hard at this time to sort out what was logical and what was not. So he began, "The house in New York is too big for just me. I'm thinking of giving it to Edward and his family. They need it, with another one on the way and all." He paused as if going on to a different angle. "The boys run the business fine. They don't need me at all now. Paul, well, he's having fun doing his own thing and I don't want to hamper that. I guess I'll take up permanent residence at Cape Charles. It's quiet there. It's smaller, and I like it." Another pause. "Yes, I guess that's what I'll do."

Arthur waited to let William think and sort, then he added, "Plus, it's half way between New York and here. That way you can go to the city for anything the boys need you for. And you do know, don't you, that you're always welcome here? There's plenty of room with Elizabeth gone and Sarah getting married soon."

William smiled weakly. "Yes, I know I am always welcome. Right now, though, this place has such a strong sense of Victoria around it. Everything I see, hear, and touch reminds me of her. That hurts."

"I understand. But the offer goes. Any time-without an invitation. After Mary and Margaret marry and leave, I expect Verna and I will be wandering around this big old house, wondering what to do with ourselves."

Then they patted each other on the backs again and just sat.

It wasn't too long after that that they noticed the lights were being extinguished, one by one. The household was settling down for the night. One light remained on-the one in the parlor.

"Come on," Arthur said to William. "He needs us."

They quietly went inside.

"Sam?" William said at the doorway to the parlor.

No response.

"Sam?" repeated Arthur.

"I'll just stay here, sir, if you don't mind."

His voice sounded deep, resigned, and tired.

Arthur, only being able to guess at the depth of pain held in Sam's heart said, "As long as you wish, son. As long as you wish."

The next morning they found him in the same chair. He was awake. William came in before anyone else and said, "Go freshen up just a little now. Go get a drink of water. Wash your face. Go to the bathroom. It'll be a long morning."

"Yes, sir." For some reason, Sam obediently followed William's directions. The household servants had warm water waiting by the time he came in from outdoors. He washed without a word to anyone. Then he returned to his seat in the parlor.

Arthur made sure the animals were taken care of. Everyone else was up now. It would be a little time before the minister arrived. The service would take place at 10:00. After that, the burial would be in the family plot, not far from the house in a shady area where Brittanhaurs had been buried for years. Arthur thought fondly of his own parents and his grandparents, who were all buried there. He also recalled the site of an infant sister of his and William. Odd that he hadn't thought about that before. He had a couple of servants go out and clean up the grave sites yesterday. Weeds were cut and fresh flowers were put on all graves. The magnolia tree that shaded them from the north wind was trimmed around. The holly bushes were trimmed so they didn't overlap or cover any stones. Everything was ready. Now it was time to just sit and wait.

He went back to the parlor and sat beside Sam. William was on the other side. The three men sat in silence, sometimes listening as the women did this, that, or the other. At other times they were lost in their own thoughts.

Quietly and little by little, people came in and sat down. Much the same group as the night before appeared. Neighbors and friends of the family took seats. The men had their hats in the hands. The ladies had their handkerchiefs in theirs.

The minister presented a brief eulogy and a sermonette. He talked about God's mercy and love. He talked about the great hope of eternal life that those had who believed in Jesus. The grave side service was shorter yet. Several people tarried to say their last good-byes. Finally, it was William and Sam. The two men stood side by side. Then, as on a cue, they turned and walked slowly back to the house. The women had shed many tears that day, but these two men remained dry eyed.

Arthur was waiting for them under the magnolia in front of the house.

"Come. Please sit for a few minutes before going in," he called.

The other two sat obediently, without a word.

"Gentlemen, contrary to popular belief, it is acceptable for men to cry. You each have suffered a great loss. I should be surprised and concerned if you didn't grieve."

A pause followed in which nobody said a word. The three men sat there.

Then Arthur broke the silence, "Sam? Perhaps you haven't thought about it yet, or perhaps you are very worried. About your future. About living here. William and I had made the contract before you and Victoria married that said in the case of divorce or death that the house and land would go back to the plantation. We never anticipated this. William and I have spoken about this, right?"

William nodded his agreement.

Arthur continued, "Sam, I don't want you to leave. Not only are you the best helper I've ever had, but I trust you with everything. I...I feel like you're a son to me. I've lost my precious niece; I don't want to lose you, too."

Now with the words said, Arthur felt better. He hadn't shown his loss like the others and now they understood why. His burden was one for the living, along with the dead.

"I thought about it a long time. If it is alright with you, I'd like to stay on at least until the harvest is in. After that, I don't know. Also, for the next, well, I don't know how long, I would like to live in the house with my parents. The other one has too many...memories, for now."

Typical of his old self, Arthur laid his hand on Sam's shoulder. "That's fine, son. Whatever you want."

That touch was what did it. Sam broke down. His sobs could have shook the world, but there, in that special place under the cover of darkness and sandwiched between two men who had become as dear to him as his own kin, Sam released the heart-wrenching burden he was bearing and shared it with them.

At one point it seemed that the door to the house opened and someone stepped out but quickly went back in again. Through their tears, though, it was hard to tell.

After a while, the release quieted itself and the men sat in darkness.

"Come on, let's go in through the kitchen door and see if we can get something to eat."

True to his word, Sam stayed that night with his parents. He stopped by his own house only long enough to get a change of clothes. He was in the barn and tending to the animals earlier than usual the next morning. He finished all the regular chores, then he went out into the fields to check on the progress of the corn, wheat, beans, tobacco, and peanuts one by one. With all that done, he mended some fence that wasn't terribly broken down, but would be soon if those hogs were let in. What he did was to keep himself busy all day. Any observer who didn't know him well would think he was just very conscientious at his job, but Sam was thinking hard. He had a lot of decisions to make. His brain seemed to work better, he thought, when his body was working, too.

That evening, after everything was done, Sam went back to his own house. He started a fire in the fireplace, even though the June air was humid even at this late hour. Then he began his task. Into the fire went the blood-stained linens, the rags and towels. Into the fire went the letters to each other that they both had kept over the years. Into the fire went the beautiful oak cradle that Sam had made with such love and care.

He sat in his chair, watching the flames lap around things; things that had once seemed precious to him he couldn't stand to see. They had to be destroyed, gone forever, just like his precious child and wife. The tears over flowed and the sobbing shook his shoulders once more. Would this pain ever end? He wondered.

Quietly, his mother slipped into the room. She sat down in the third chair in the room, purposefully leaving the one that Victoria sat in free. "I saw the smoke first, then the flames shooting out the top. Your Dad was terribly worried, but I knew you wouldn't do anything stupid. No. But I understand your pain, son. I know. I've lost loved ones, too. Now, you do what you need to do. But when you're done, you come on down to the house and get yourself something to eat and you rest. You've worked yourself hard today-physically and mentally-and I know you're exhausted. But consider this. Someday you might want to hold something in your hand, hold it to your heart, that she held once in hers. It might help to feel her touch, smell her scent, and see her face. Think, son."

Sam never looked up from the fire. He had gathered other things near him to throw in-the curtains, the pillowcases Victoria was so fond of embroidering on, the vase she loved to keep flowers in, and more.

Ann slipped out of the room as quietly as she had come in. Caught in his own reverie, Sam didn't even notice, but he didn't put anything else on the fire. When the flames burned down some, he looked up and rubbed his eyes. Was that a dream or a vision? Had his mother really been there and spoken to him?

He realized he was exceedingly tired. So he spread out the wood so the fire would die down. Gathering up some clean clothes, he blew out the lone lantern he had lit and walked out the door, shutting it softly behind him.

Sam stayed with his parents for a few more nights without going back to his house at all. In the meantime, though, Ann had been very busy. She had been up to the house. She cleaned it all, room by room. She re-hung the curtains, re-made the bed with fresh linens, and re-stocked the pantry. Everything would be in order for when her son was ready to go home.

She thought a lot as she worked. It was good for Sam to be staying with her and Javan. She knew he didn't need to be alone right now, and even though he didn't say much, he was still good company to them. It was nice to have one of their children in the house again, but she knew, as every mother does, that at some time each child has to go out on his own. Like little birds, she thought, the image reminding her of Victoria. They have to test their wings and learn how to fly. Then they're gone.

The thought reminded her of her youngest three boys. They had been doing very well at the photography business. So well, in fact, that two of them, James and Ben, had met nice young ladies whose families were well off enough to afford photographs frequently. She suspected the two of them would court and marry those girls soon. As for Walter, he needed to prove himself. Odd, she thought, as he was the one who learned and started the business in the first place. He seemed to want to move on. Perhaps the area was too reminiscent of the accident that lost him his eye and arm. He had been talking of moving recently. If he did, she hoped it wouldn't be too far away. She would miss him. She was grateful that all her children lived nearby. They were far enough away to be on their own, yet close enough to come visit regularly. That was just right, she thought, and as it should be.

Sam walked past his house twice a day, once in the morning on the way to the plantation and again in the evening when he came home. But one evening about a week after the funeral, he noticed the windows were open and the curtains were flapping in the breeze.

"What in the world?" he thought to himself, wondering at first if some vagrant had taken up residence.

He walked up to the porch. No lights on. He opened the door and went inside. The first thing that he noticed was the fresh scent. Everything was clean. No more smell of blood and death. He lit the lantern and walked throughout the house. Everything was inviting. The clean floors. The chairs in place before the fire. The clean bedding. The clothes hanging on the peg. The stocked pantry. Then he knew he needed to come home. Then he knew that as much as the pain of Victoria's death hurt, he could go on. He could live in this house and hold her memory sacred. He didn't need to run from her ghost anymore. He could live with it and share this house with it. For the first time in over a week, he smiled.

He strolled quickly the rest of the way down the lane to Javan and Ann's house. He strolled in with a purposefulness to his step that hadn't been there for a while.

"Good evening, son" both his parents said in their usual way.

He walked over to his mother, kissed her cheek, and whispered, "Thank you, Mom."

With that he gathered up his few belongings and went back out the door. He went home.

CHAPTER 10

▼

THE DECISION

The harvest that year was acceptable. It wasn't the extraordinary harvest like the one several years prior, but it was acceptable. Sam counted again the paper money from his share of the profits. It was enough to go out on his own. It wasn't enough to buy a farm, but enough to get started somewhere doing something. He wondered where and what.

Walter and Ben didn't need help in their photography studio. James was there to handle all the book keeping, and besides, Sam didn't have a head for either of those things.

Captain Charlie could use help with his fishing business, but Sam just couldn't see himself floating his days away. Besides, he knew he could help with transporting eels to New York City, but he wasn't sure he wanted to keep in close contact with the places that held so many memories of Victoria and her family.

He knew William could find a place for him in one of his many business ventures, but he wasn't a businessman. Wearing suits and living in the city did not appeal to him in the least.

Richard was still working in his grocery store and he didn't need any extra help or responsibilities.

Robert was doing well on his farm, but with a wife, four children, and his own servants, he didn't need any more help. Besides, he was the oldest, the most independent, and Sam felt that of all his siblings Robert was the one he got along with least well.

That left his sister, as far as contacts went. Rosa's husband Joseph was doing well as a special agent on the New York, Philadelphia and Norfolk Railroad. He probably wasn't in a position to hire anyone to work under him, but Sam wondered if he would be able to recommend him for some starting position. Sam recalled the first time he and Victoria had taken the train to New York. He loved it! He remembered saying that he thought he could ride a train every day and never tire of it. Yes, that was his answer. He would ask Joseph if there were any positions available on any of the train lines he knew of.

Having logically thought through his prospects, Sam was stolid in his decision. His mind made up, he decided to go speak to Arthur. He knew this would be the hard part, as he knew Arthur would do his best to talk him out of leaving.

"Sam, I will admit my first instinct is to try to talk you out of this plan. My heart hurts so at the thought of you leaving. We've been through so much together. You're family now, not just a hired hand. In fact, poor old Frank is down with the gout again and I was thinking of offering you the position of foreman around here. But, son, I can see that your mind is made up." Arthur said after Sam told him his plan.

Sam nodded. He felt every affection for the older man and his family, also. It would be hard to leave, especially during the holidays.

"But, Sam, I understand. I understand your need to start again. You are always welcome to stay in the house you're in, as long as you like."

Sam thanked the older man who had become a second father to him. He thought about the odd twists of fate. He had his own parents still living, and his own brothers and sister. Then there were all the Brittanhaurs who were as close to him as blood relation could be. And yet, he felt so alone in the world. He knew he could not be content farming the land anymore. It was time for a change-a drastic change.

He had spoken to Rosa and Joseph the previous Sunday afternoon at his parent's house. Joseph had promised to check into possibilities for him and let him know as soon as possible if anything came up.

True to his word, his brother-in-law came by that following evening.

"Hey, Joseph, it's only Monday. You work fast!" Sam started as he welcomed Joseph into his house.

"Well, I did a little asking around today and I found you a job, if you want it. One of the guys got hurt over the weekend and it looks like he won't be back for a while. They need someone to fill his place immediately, so you could start as early as tomorrow. I took the liberty of telling them that you would take it. What do you think?"

Joseph was a very personable man but was also business-like and serious when need be. Sam couldn't imagine what it would be like to work with him, so they talked about what the job involved. The position was of a mechanic working in the shop. The previous man had slipped while working on some wheels and one had rolled over his leg, crushing the bones. He was sure to be out for quite some time.

Sam thought about it for a minute then asked, "This will all be new to me, Joseph. Will you show me the ropes?"

"Well, of course. That's not an area I work in, but, I tell you what. Why don't you come home with me tonight and stay with us? I'll take you over early in the morning to show you around and then introduce you to the shop foreman."

Joseph knew Sam had been through a lot in the last six months. Rosa, much like her mother, had a big heart, and had told Joseph about how she thought Sam must be hurting. She wanted to help her younger brother all she could. Joseph knew it would make her happy to help him, plus he also knew it was the right thing to do.

Sam packed a few things he thought he might need in a bag. The two men had to go past Sunbury to get to Joseph's house, so they would stop on the way and tell Arthur what was going on.

Arthur and Verna were sitting in the parlor when Sam and Joseph came up. Arthur's heart immediately sank as he suspected what this evening visit meant. Verna, unaware of former conversations about jobs, was shocked when Sam told them what he was doing. She began to cry.

"But, Sam, haven't we always treated you like our own son? Haven't you been happy here?" she wailed between sobs.

Going over to her, he took her hands and said, "Yes, ma'am. You have always treated me better than I ever could have imagined. But without Victoria here, I feel like I'm only half here. Her memories haunt me. Please understand that I'm not unhappy about you, or your husband, or the work. I'm unhappy about me."

She stood and hugged him, drying her tears. "I understand. You are always welcome here. I love you."

They hugged and he whispered in her ear, "I love you, too, Aunt Verna, but I've got to go."

Arthur and Verna waved from the door as Sam and Joseph went down the road. Then Verna turned to Arthur and hugged him for support. "All our children are leaving us, aren't they?"

"Yes, dear. That is as it should be."

CHAPTER 11

▼

THE NEW BEGINNING

Sam found his new job exciting. It was fun to learn something new and to be stretching his mind again. He was glad to have his hands busy. He found himself thinking less about his precious wife and child every day. During the week, he stayed with his sister and Joseph in their house near the train yard. On Fridays after work he would walk to The Bird's Nest. He would always make a point to stop at his parent's house on Saturday to talk about his week and theirs. Then he usually spent Sunday afternoons at Sunbury before heading back to Rosa and Joseph's house. After a few weeks, he remembered that Christmas was coming.

Rosa and Joseph enjoyed having him stay with them, but they also knew how important family was to him. They convinced him that anything he wanted to do for the holidays was fine with them. He could even invite others to their house. Sam thought about it then asked Arthur one Sunday afternoon, "Sir, do you think that William will be at Cape Charles for the holidays?"

Arthur was mildly surprised at the question. "Yes, he will. He has invited us over for the week following Christmas. He knew we would want to be here with the girls and have them all in on Christmas day. I had invited him here, but you know how he dislikes huge gatherings."

"Do you think he'd mind if I dropped in on him?" Sam asked.

"No! I'm sure he'd welcome a visit from you!"

So it was decided that Sam would go over on Christmas Day and the Brittanhaurs would go the day after that.

As Arthur suspected, William was glad to see Sam. The older man had a ham in the oven and chuckled when Sam smelled the aroma from the kitchen.

"Yes, I've learned to be quite a good cook in the past year," he said. "I'm glad to see you and to have someone to share this ham with me. I'm not much for turkey, so I figured I could break with tradition and have whatever I wanted."

Sam smiled. Yes, he had felt the same over the last six months. Sometimes he sat down, too tired to fix a decent meal for himself and grabbed whatever happened to be available at the time. That was at his own home. At Rosa's house, she made sure he ate well. She packed him a good lunch, too. He had read about miners and the way their wives fixed their lunches and how they had to eat in the dark of the mines. He was glad at that point that he worked on top of the soil instead of under it.

"Sir?" he started.

"Yes, Sam," William always gave him his full attention, as if every word he said bore specific importance.

"We have a lot to be thankful for."

"Yes, Sam. You are right. The last 13 months have been very difficult for both of us. But you and I are the type to keep going. We understand about life…and death."

Sam stayed the night at the house in Cape Charles. He slept in the bed that he and Victoria used to sleep in. He missed her warmth, her scent, everything about her, but the pain was less. He could sleep now without reaching out to make sure she was covered. He could sleep without the nightmares stealing his rest.

The next morning, Sam left early to cross the bay.

William had walked with him to the dock, and it was William who broke the silence,

"Thank you, son, for coming to spend the day with me."

They shook hands, hugged, patting each other on the back like in olden times. "Good luck to you, Sam."

"And to you, Sir."

They neither one knew that would be the last they would see of each other.

Sam proved himself to be an excellent mechanic. That was something Arthur had known even when Sam was a teen and first began to work for him. So it came as no surprise to anyone who knew him that he moved up in the shop quickly. By the end of February he was no longer a common laborer, but rather a skilled mechanic specializing in wheels. By June he was working on more complex things, like the engines themselves. Sam found the work tiring, but fulfilling.

One Friday afternoon he walked toward Sunbury and noticed a placard in a front door. The house, a large Victorian house only four blocks from the train yard, had a room for rent. He went up to the door and knocked.

The elderly lady who opened the door answered his questions about room and board. She explained that her own son had recently married and moved out of the house. With a room unused and finding it harder and harder to make ends meet, she had decided to rent it out.

Sam found the lady to be motherly and he felt sorry for her predicament. So he decided to let the room. He would move in the following Monday. That gave him time to visit at Sunbury and gather his things.

Telling his parents was not difficult. He offered to let them have anything they needed or wanted from his house. His mother quietly asked to have Victoria's vase. She commented that it would remind her of the good times the two of them used to have in their gardens.

Rosa and Joseph came to get the bedstead. They were expecting again and could move their older child from the crib to a bed now, in preparation for the new baby. All the other furniture had come with the house. Sam wondered if there was anything that William might want, so when he went to Sunbury on Sunday afternoon, as usual. He first told them about his new place, then inquired if there was anything else Arthur or Verna needed him to do around there to close up shop

Arthur and Verna heartily agreed, "No, Sam. You have done so much for us, we could never repay you. You have cleared land, tended animals and fields, repaired your house and your parent's, and…well, too much more to even begin telling of all that you've done."

Verna added, "You know you're always welcome to come here. You can stay in the house with us. There's plenty of room now."

Sam thanked the couple for all they had done for him. He reassured them that he would be back and asked that they let William know what he was doing. Arthur assured him that William could have any remembrances of his daughter's that he wanted from the house and that he would keep in touch.

Sam said good-bye with a hug to both of them, then he took one more trip to the cemetery. He had picked jonquils which were just starting to bloom on southern facing ditches to place on the grave of his wife and daughter. Then he started toward town to start a new chapter in his life.

CHAPTER 12

▼

THE CHANGES

Sam was happy living at Miss Edith's, as he called her. She was a pleasant old lady who enjoyed his company. Often she would have some special dish fixed for supper when he got home from work. She was a good cook and she quickly figured out which dishes were his favorites. Sam suspected she rented out the room more to have company in the house than for the need for money, but he paid his rent on time each month, and the two soon became quick friends. Miss Edith discovered Sam's ability to fix anything and soon had him tinkering around the house. The odd jobs, she told him, would apply toward his rent. But he didn't mind doing them. It gave him something to do on the weekends and he didn't mind helping the old lady out with things she wasn't able to do for herself.

He wondered what her life was like while he was away at work. She simply stated, "Mondays I wash clothes. Tuesdays I iron and put them away. Wednesdays I go to Women's Circle, a church group that learns about missions and makes things like quilts to send to poor people around the country. Thursdays I run my errands and do whatever needs to be done. Fridays I clean. Saturdays I bake. Sundays are church and rest. What else is there?"

Sam laughed good-naturedly. She was right. Her week was very busy and she seemed to thrive on the routineness. Sam, though, was a breath of fresh air for her. He would tell her the news of the train yard and anything else he knew from around town.

In June Sam made a trip out to Sunbury to place flowers on the grave. He looked around. Everything seemed to be in order, but nobody was home. He figured that the Brittanhaurs had gone across the bay to Cape Charles to see William. He also figured his own parents had gone to visit some brother or sister of his. So he wasn't too startled at finding himself alone. He thought about stopping at his former home, but decided against it at this time. Next time, he thought.

November came and so did a promotion. The people over him had noticed how useful he was involving anything mechanical. Another man had recently retired, after 50 years of service. So Sam moved up to shop foreman. It involved a raise in pay. Sam decided to treat himself to a set of new clothes. Virdie had always taken care of all that for him, and after a year and a half, he was in need of some new things.

That evening he told Miss Edith, "Please don't fix any supper for us for Friday night. I am taking you out."

"What? Now young man, it just ain't fittin' for a..." she started to protest.

"Now Miss Edith, you have been so good to me. When was the last time you went out anywhere fancy? His eyes twinkled and she knew she was going to give in to him.

"Alright. I will be ready with my best dress on." she already looked forward to this unexpected outing.

"That's right and I'll wear my suit. We will shop a little first, if you don't mind. I need more work clothes. After that we will find a place to dine. If you have any preferences, it's my treat." Sam told her the general idea and left the details up to her. After all, she was a native of the town and he expected her to know the area.

Friday night came and Sam bathed and changed clothes quickly before they left the house. He had a pocketful of money from his first pay check at his new job. It felt good to be out and looking at the sites of the town. Edith was a good tour guide. She pointed out friends' homes, certain shops and all their idiosyncrasies, and several landmarks. She took Sam to a perfect place for men's clothes and he bought himself the clothes he needed. Then they went to eat. They walked with Edith on Sam's arm and the two of them laughed gaily as they strolled along the streets of Norfolk. They window shopped at the closed stores, stopping to admire some trinket or new invention. Sam would comment on the prices or utility of some items, and Edith commented on the quality or the beauty of others.

"Sam, what will people think of the two of us like this?" Edith questioned.

"Do you think I care, Edith? If you do, you can tell them whatever you wish. I am your long-lost nephew visiting from Buffalo. I am your illegitimate son visiting from Paris. I am your youngest brother just in from Kalamazoo or Timbuktu. Or perhaps I am your live-in boy friend." He laughed at the outrageous ideas and that he had even suggested them.

Edith, always good natured, too, said, "I think the last one will raise some eyebrows. What will my church ladies think?" Then she giggled and they strolled on.

At the gate to her house, Edith turned to Sam and said, "That was the most fun I've had in a long time. Thank you, Sam, for a lovely evening."

With a flourishing bow, he said, "The pleasure was mine, madam. May I see you to your door?" Then the pair went in.

Christmas came and went. Sam spent it with Edith, who would have been alone otherwise. She fixed them a turkey meal with all the trimmings. They set up a Christmas tree in the parlor and Edith found some decorations in the attic that she had forgotten about for years. On Christmas Day, the two of them exchanged tokens of the affection between them. Edith had bought a watch for Sam. It was a beautiful pocket watch with a train on the cover.

"Oh, Edith!" he cried. "I love this. It is perfect and you mark my words. Some day I will drive one of these things."

Edith smiled at the thought of Sam behind a powerful locomotive. "I know you will," she smiled fondly.

Then she opened her present from him. It was a lovely silk scarf and matching brooch. He had seen her admiring it in a store window on the Friday evening they had gone out. He had slipped back the following week after work and had hidden it all these weeks.

"Sam! How did you know I had my eye on this?" The elderly lady was almost in tears as she fingered the fine filigree of the brooch. "It's beautiful."

"Here. Let me pin it on you." He put the scarf around her neck and pinned it in place with the brooch. Although it didn't match her dress, she didn't care. It was a lovely token of his fondness for her, and that made it more special than matching her dress. The following Sunday, though, found her wearing a dress that did match. Off she went to church, ready to show off her finery from Christmas. Sam just chuckled as she went out the door. He had truly become fond of the old lady and realized that several days had gone by without thinking about Victoria and the baby. He surprised himself to think that he had actually been happy without her. It was a happiness marred by their absence, and nothing could fill the void in his heart that their deaths left with him. But at least every day wasn't an exercise in purposeful forgetfulness as it had been before. Sam allowed himself to wonder if he would ever love another woman as he had loved Virdie. Then he thought of Miss Edith and smiled to himself.

January of 1907 was one of the worst anyone could remember. Snow storm followed ice storm followed snow storm. Roads were closed. Rivers were frozen shut. Many means of transportation were shut down. At this time Sam was glad that he wasn't working on the train itself but rather in the shop. The shop doors could be closed and the coal and oil stoves kept the building warm. He saw the men coming in off the trains. Some had sleet and snow frozen to their faces. Some complained of hands and feet being frozen. And yet, something drew him to the steaming, smoking engines. It was true that their sounds assaulted the air. Their smoke and ashes belched forth, spreading filth onto everyone and everything near. But just as some men become addicted to alcohol, Sam felt he was becoming addicted to the iron giants that moved on rails. He was intrigued by everything about them. So he began to read.

He told Miss Edith about his increasing interest in steam and rail transportation. She commented that she walked past the library every time she went to church. She would stop the next day and get him a book on the subject. Over the next few months Sam read everything Edith could bring home about trains. It wasn't too long before he understood all the inner workings of the engine. He read about the history, too. From the Tom Thumb and Best Friend of Charleston to the Golden Spike at Promontory Point, Utah, and beyond. Sam would sit in the evenings in front of the fireplace, book in hand. Edith would sit, too, some needlework in hand. The two of them were often quiet, but many times Sam would share his new knowledge with his landlady. She seemed to enjoy the learning. "Learn something new every day," she would say. "That's the only way to keep from getting stagnant."

Sam appreciated her willingness to be enthusiastic about anything he was interesting in, and he realized how much a part of her life he had become. He wouldn't dare think of moving. Besides, the location was convenient to work, and the price of the rent was right. So, for now, he foresaw no changes in his situation.

Another year went by. Christmas came again. Sam reflected that he had gone back to Sunbury only once, to place flowers on the grave in June. He had stopped to talk briefly to Arthur, who told him that both Mary and Margaret were married and gone now. He also said that William had met a woman at church that he was becoming increasingly fond of, and Arthur thought that the two elderly people would probably marry soon.

"William married again?" Sam thought to himself as he walked back home. The idea seemed so incongruous that Sam just shook his head.

The following January was mild. Everyone commented on what a difference it was from the previous year. But they should have known it was just the calm before the storm. February came in like a lion. Like in the year before, one storm barely exited the area before another came along. Each dumped snow and ice on the tired region. Edith insisted on going to church each Wednesday and Sunday, sometimes turning around and coming back because nobody else was there.

Sam noticed her cough in late February. "Edith, you have done it now. You've been out in that cold and now you have a cough. What am I going to do with you?" Sam joked, not realizing how serious this would become.

"Bring some honey and rum tea and then we'll see," she teased in return.

Sam brought her tea, but chamomile, not honey and rum. Over the next week, though, the cough got worse. It sounded like it changed from her throat to deep in her chest. That's when Sam began to worry.

"Edith, I don't feel comfortable leaving you alone today. Is there anyone who would come in and sit with you while I'm at work?" Sam began one early morning.

"Yes. The Pope would be glad to come, as would the president. They are dear friends of mine and have been waiting for you to get out of here so they could come exploit an old woman."

Sam shook his head at the way she feistily cared on, even when apparently very ill.

"Edith, I'm serious. Your son? Someone from church?"

"No," now she was serious. "There's no one. My son lives in Richmond, you know. You go on to work and I will stay in today. I'll wait right here for you. Then I'll beat you at cribbage tonight."

Sam reluctantly left the house for work. She was a spunky gal, he had to admit. He also wondered what had happened between Edith and her son to make them lose contact. She seemed so enjoyable that he couldn't imagine having a falling out with her. He wondered if he should try to contact her son somehow to tell him of his mother's condition.

That day at work Sam asked around about how he could contact Edith's son. One man suggested calling information on the telephone. That might just work, he thought, but who did he know who had a phone?

That evening Edith did not greet him at the door. Instead, she was wrapped in a quilt and sitting as near the fire as she dare. Sam had made sure she had plenty of fire wood available within close reach before he left every morning. But it appeared that she hadn't done much throughout the day, which was highly unlike her.

"Edith," Sam began after he had fixed them some supper and she had eaten a little, "be serious with me now. I think your son ought to know how ill you are. I can contact him. The Brittanhaurs have a phone at Sunbury. I can call him on the telephone. Please. I think you're very ill."

"No!" she almost shouted. "He doesn't care about me! All he cares about is that floozy girl he married. She tricked him into it, you know. I was against it from the start. With all her lace and heels and fancy hair. She wasn't a good girl. She stole him from me. She…"

Edith stopped, winded. Sam could see that the emotion had gotten the best of her and she was exhausted. "Come now," he said. "You're going to bed."

He helped her get up the stairs and made sure she was warmly tucked in with plenty of quilts before he blew out the candle and went to his own room. He laid there in the darkness, trying to sort out what to do. He came to appreciate the relationship he had with all the Brittanhaurs. He couldn't imagine feeling so much anger toward someone married into the family. How sad, he thought. Sam vowed to visit Arthur and Verna soon. He vowed to visit William again. And his own parents. It had been a long time since he had seen them, too.

The next day, a Saturday, Sam made the trek to Sunbury. He stopped to visit with Arthur and Verna for all morning. He stayed for lunch and he did use their telephone. He was able to find Edith's son in Richmond and told him of her illness. He seemed to want to come, but said a lot depended on his wife. "She's not in any condition to travel," Sam was told. Sam wondered if that meant she was pregnant, but didn't ask. That afternoon Sam visited with his parents. He was surprised to see how much they had aged. His mother, in particular, seemed more grey, wrinkled, and hunched than ever before. Hard work outside had crept up on her.

He had a pleasant visit with all of them. Before going back to Edith, he stopped at the cemetery. "Virdie?" he began. "I know I haven't been here to see you for a while. I'm doing fine. I work hard. I'm moving up in the world. You would've been proud. I miss you. Good-bye, little one."

These words had come slowly and haltingly. Sam was in no hurry. He felt some obligation to linger at the grave. Then he headed toward town. Edith's pastor was supposed to have come to visit her that day, and Sam didn't particularly want to be in the house while he was there. He had met the man before and had found him to be a soft-handed, smooth-tongued marshmallow. Sam recalled Victoria describing some of her suitors in New York that way. She had always used a tone of utter disgust when talking about them and Sam now knew why. He had rarely met anyone who fit that description, but this pastor did to a T.

As he turned in the sidewalk at the house, he noticed that a lot of lights were on. Going in, he found the pastor still there. His wife was busy in the kitchen, and the doctor was in the bedroom with Edith.

"What is going on here?" he said in a voice that sounded rougher than he intended.

"We could ask you the same thing, young man," the pastor retorted. His wife nodded agreement from the kitchen doorway. "Edith has pneumonia. She should have been in the hospital days ago. Now the doctor thinks it would do more damage to move her, so he is treating her here."

With that the doctor came down the stairs. He was a quieter and calmer man. "I'm Dr. Winslow," he introduced himself. "Let's talk."

He took Sam into the parlor. Sam was secretly hoping it would be just the two of them, but the pastor and his wife followed as if they owned the place.

"Edith is very sick," the doctor began. "She has pneumonia and needs bed rest. I have set up pots in her room to put warm, wet air all around her. Your job will be to check those throughout the night. It is important that the air not get cold or dry. That could kill her."

"I understand. I will do my best," Sam replied with conviction.

"Fine. I will be back tomorrow morning around 9:00. Good night."

The doctor seemed very businesslike or aloof. Sam couldn't tell which. He thought that perhaps he was just tired-maybe tired of dealing with the pastor and his wife. All three packed up and left. Sam bounded up the stairs to Edith's room.

"There you are! You gave me such a scare!" she croaked, unable to speak much louder than a whisper.

"I gave you a scare! You gave me a scare!" Sam realized that she would joke and tease with him to the very end. It was the way their relationship was.

They talked for a while and Sam left the room only to get more water for the pots or coals for the fires under them. The room was hot and humid and Sam asked permission to take off his shirt.

"Go ahead," Edith whispered. "Maybe the sight will make my blood pressure go up and I'll get well!"

They smiled together. Sam sat in a wooden chair near her bed. Eventually they both fell asleep, but as he promised, Sam kept the pots filled and the fires going all night.

The next morning the doctor arrived to check on his patient. Both Sam and he agreed that it was pleasant without the pastor and his wife interfering. They laughed together quietly. Then he checked Edith. "She's no better, but she's also no worse," was his prognosis for the day. "Keep her quiet and in bed and I'll check on her tomorrow at the same time."

So Edith and Sam spent a quiet day at home. It was the first time in years that she had missed church, she told Sam. Sam secretly cringed to think of receiving spiritual instruction from that weasel-faced whiner, but Edith assured him that he was a knowledgeable man in his field. "Just never had to be rough," she told him.

Around 11:00 Edith requested that Sam read to her from her Bible. "Start with Psalm 23." Sam read it aloud. Then Deuteronomy 28. It was a longer passage, but Edith said it was one of her favorites. Now I Corinthians 13. They jumped around reading favorite verses and chapters from here and there. They talked about Jonah, Isaac, Paul, and Moses. Sam found Edith to be very knowledgeable about the Bible and enjoyed her insight. It seemed to him when they looked up and the clock said 2:00 that he had learned more from the Bible in those three hours than he had in years of church attendance.

"I'll get us some soup," he said. First he refilled the water pots and the coal burners. After a little while he returned with chicken noodle soup. They ate in silence, Edith only eating a few spoonfuls. The rest of the afternoon was spent in quiet chatting and napping. Around 6:00 Sam thought he heard a knock at the door. He went downstairs to find a man about his own age, height, and build at the door.

"Hello. I'm John, Edith's son. How is my mother?"

Sam was so taken aback that he forgot his manners for a moment. When he recovered, he invited John in and told him of her condition. "Do you want to see her? Of course, you do, otherwise why would you be here?"

Over the next few hours Sam watched a miracle take place. John told his mother how he had married his wife just to spite her. He realized later that she was a drunkard and a loose woman. John had asked her for a divorce just the day before. John asked his mother for forgiveness, and she willingly gave it. After three hours of talking, Edith asked, "Why did you come now?"

"Sam called and told me how bad off you were. It was then that I knew I had to make that decision to totally break it off from Delilah. She wouldn't have let me come to see you, you know. She was always jealous of our relationship."

"I'm glad you're here, son," whispered Edith. It was evident that she was very tired, but she mustered enough strength to stretch her hand toward Sam, "Thank you, you rascally young man."

She drifted off to sleep. Sam went to his own room to sleep and let John spend the night with his mother, instructing him about the importance of the pots of water and the fires.

The next morning Sam did not hear any stirring in Edith's room, so he assumed that she and her son were still asleep. Sam tip-toed down the stairs, thinking that it was very good for John to be there with her while he went to work. He knew the doctor would arrive at 9:00 and he hoped that he would find her condition better. She seemed to be in good spirits the night before.

Sam worked hard that day, repairing some engines that had worn out during the previous storms. Plus, late in the day, he was called to the manager's office.

"Sam," the manager said, "your work has been outstanding. You are efficient and well versed on all the engines and all parts of the engines. We in management feel that we could put your expertise to better use elsewhere. What would you think of becoming an engineer?"

Sam stood in amazement. Most men had to start as brakeman or fireman and work their way up to engineer or conductor. He was being offered a job he really coveted. What luck!

"Yes, sir. I would like that job very much."

"Great!" the manager replied. "You will train for the next month. You will work one week with a brakeman and one week with a fireman, just so that you understand what each of those jobs involve. Then you will be alongside an experienced engineer who plans to retire soon. You will work with him for two weeks. After that, we will test run you with another engineer for two weeks. At the end of that time, you should get a train of your own."

Sam was so elated that he ran home. "What a lucky day," he thought to himself. "I will tell Edith that my dreams are coming true. She'll be better and she'll say in her feisty way "I told you so.'"

But Sam's trot screeched to a halt as he rounded the corner in front of Edith's block. A long, dark wagon was in front of the house. Many lights were on. He raced up to the door and threw it open.

Blocking the doorway was the pastor. He tried to hold Sam back, but the small, soft man was no match for Sam's bulk and strength. Sam ran through the house till he found John.

"What is going on here?" he practically yelled.

"Mom died in the night, Sam," he sniffled. "I didn't keep the pots going like you told me. She started coughing and couldn't get her breath. Then she calmed down. I thought it was just a fit or something. When the doctor arrived in the morning, I let him in. He said she had been dead for several hours. I thought she was just resting quietly. I didn't know. Really."

Sam headed for the parlor. Nothing. The kitchen. Nothing.

"Where is she?" he shouted.

The pastor pointed toward the wagon out front. "The funeral director will take care of her. We'll have a viewing tomorrow night at the church and the funeral will be Wednesday in the morning. Right, John?"

Sam thought how perfectly the pastor and John seemed to work together. He found himself disgusted by their oily mannerisms, so he went up to his room, gathered up his few belongings, and headed toward Rosa and Joseph's house. It wasn't until then that he realized the wagon out front was actually a hearse. He had an over-whelming desire to peak in, but out of respect for the dead, he didn't.

At Rosa and Joseph's he was welcomed with open arms. They hadn't seen him for a long time, so he tried to give them an abbreviated version of his life since leaving their home. He finished with his victory of the day-gaining a new position-and his defeat-losing a dear friend.

Joseph assured him that he would be able to take Wednesday morning off from work. "They are a very understanding group of people," he said. "Many people on the railroad get injured or killed. We're like a big family. We help each other whenever and however we can."

Sam felt better for having come there. It was good to be with family again, and it was good to be with Joseph, who knew about the railroad more than he.

Tuesday found Sam tired, but he performed his duties with an efficiency and diligence typical of his work every day. So no one knew anything was the matter. That afternoon, before leaving for Rosa and Joseph's home, Sam went to the manager. He told him what had happened the previous day and requested the morning off so that he could attend the funeral. Permission was quickly given, and then the manager asked, "So where are you living now?"

Sam told him about his brother-in-law and sister, but the manager commented, "You know, let me ask around. When you come back tomorrow afternoon, come see me first before going to the shop. I may have another surprise for you."

Sam attended Edith's funeral, being sure to sit near the back of the church. Fortunately, the graveyard was behind the church. The little group walked there, following the casket bearers. The grave side ceremony, like the sermon inside the church, had been filled with lofty references to scriptures, but Sam felt none of the inspiration that he had on Sunday while sharing verses with Edith. What she ever saw in this man, he could only guess.

After the service, the people were invited for sandwiches and tea at the parsonage. Although he was hungry, Sam declined, saying that he needed to get back to work. As he was walking toward the gate, John caught up with him.

"Uh, Sam, can we talk for a few minutes?" John inquired.

"I'm sorry, John. I really need to get back to work."

"What about this evening?" John persisted.

"Well, I really need to find another place to live." Sam felt like a leach had attached itself to him and he couldn't get it off, no matter how hard he shook or pulled.

"No you don't." John said, almost under his breath.

"What? If you have something to say, speak up and quit wasting my time!" The emotions of the last few days came out in his tone of voice and made his speech short and strained, a rare occasion for Sam

"Alright! My mother left the house and all its contents to you. I get the money in the bank and the family business." John spurted like a fountain.

"What?" Sam shook his head to clear it.

The two men went into the foyer of the church to get out of the wind while they talked. "It seems she wrote a new will last year while she and I were at odds with each other. You were a comfort and a joy to her. I don't begrudge you that at all. I'm glad you were there. It seems you took better care of her at the end than I did, and I will always regret that. But, legally, and yes, I have already checked into it, you own the house and its contents, free and clear. The family business and the money in the bank goes to me."

"What family business was that?" Sam asked, unaware that there was one.

"Well, Taliaferro's, of course."

Sam recognized the name. Pronounced Tolliver, it was a prominent name in the Suffolk and Norfolk area. John quickly filled in the details. His grandfather and then his father had run a store in the downtown Norfolk area for years. At first it was a general store, then his father had refined its business to clothing, including hats, purses, and jewelry. The business had boomed. His parents were quite well to do. Everything they made, though, went in the bank. John was expected to take over the business when he was older, but he had run off with Delilah. His father had died years before, and the business was run by a manager who was probably in his 70's. He had been a faithful family friend for many years.

Sam was amazed. That was the same store Edith had taken him to when he needed clothes. It was the same store where he bought her the scarf and brooch she so admired. It was amazing that she never let on. As the pieces of a puzzle fell into place, Sam saw things in a different light. So Edith really didn't need the income from the rent of the room. She needed company. She had been a delightful, interesting lady who liked to live her own way and say her mind. She had been shunned for those qualities by the social elites of Norfolk and she preferred to spend her time coddling Sam and his interests. He had never put two and two together. He wondered at how blind he had been, but then, rather than beat himself up about it, he contented himself with the thought that God had been in control. The old lady needed him and he had needed the old lady. With a smile and a shake of the head, Sam walked back to work, stopping at the manager's office to tell him that he didn't need a home after all.

"That's great," the manager said, "because what I thought was a sure thing for you fell through. Odd how things work out sometimes, isn't it?"

"Always for the best," Sam said. "Always for the best."

Rosa and Joseph were disappointed that Sam wasn't going to be spending more time with them, but they were amazed and happy for him at the announcement of owning his own home. This was a first for Sam, and he spent his weekends from then on doing all those home improvements that seem to never end when you own a house. He also decided to make a little plaque for out front of the house that said "Welcome to the Bird's Nest." It was his way of keeping a piece of Virdie alive and with him. This would remind him of her.

He took what clothes and belongings of Edith's that neither he nor John wanted and took them to a local orphanage. There were usable clothes, among other things. Sam made sure, though, that the scarf and brooch he bought her stayed in the house. They would be a special remembrance of Edith.

CHAPTER 13

▼

THE TRAINING

By the next Monday, Sam felt settled into Edith's house, although he began referring to it as "The Bird's Nest" to others. Soon it became well known as that, partially because Sam put up bird houses and bird feeders of every shape and size everywhere possible in an attempt to encourage the birds to come and stay.

Sam threw himself into his training of the different jobs on a locomotive. First he trained with the brakeman. He wondered that these men weren't better paid, for surely their jobs were the hardest and the most dangerous. Next came the fireman. This was a dirty job that involved a lot of stooping, lifting, and scooping. Sam went home very tired during those days, but he had to admit that he enjoyed learning something new. He also knew that Edith, along with Victoria and the baby, were smiling down on him.

The weather had turned warm and Spring was just around the corner. Sam felt so good about himself and his position in life that he invited his whole family to come to his house for Easter Sunday dinner. He puttered about the house all day the Saturday before, putting jonquils in vases in all the window sills, dusting even the tops of door jambs, and mopping floors that didn't need to be mopped. He fretted and stewed like an old mother hen, he thought to himself. But this was important. He was going to show his family how far he had come and that he could make it on his own.

Easter Sunday dawned bright and clear, if not crisp and a little breezy. Sam went to a sunrise service nearby, but not at Edith's church. Then he made it home before any of his guests arrived. Not too long afterward, though, his brothers started trickling in. Ben and James had news. Walter had taken a job in Charleston, South Carolina. He had moved just the week before and he had called to tell them that he was doing well and enjoyed the warm weather. They were jealous of that, but were hesitant to tell their mother. This was the farthest away any of her brood had moved, and they knew it would upset her.

"Perhaps her loss will be overshadowed by your successes," Ben commented. James agreed. Sam could only hope so. He knew how much family meant to his mother, and this was sure to be a shock.

Little by little, his large family filled his house. It was fun, though, he realized, to hear the house bursting with noise and laughter. The nieces and nephews played outside after the meal. Javan and Ann looked around the entire house with appreciation and obvious approval.

"Yes, son," Javan said, "We always knew you'd make good. We knew all our children would. You are all fine children and are joys to our hearts."

That was about as much of a speech as Javan had ever made. After that, he sat down in a rocker on the back porch and watched the grandchildren playing till he dozed off.

Ann helped Sam in the kitchen. "Everything was wonderful, son. I don't know how you pulled off such a fine meal for so many people!"

"I learned from the best, mother. I learned from you." Sam replied.

She leaned against him and gave him a hug. "I'm real proud of you, Sam. You've come a long way."

Sam knew what she meant. He turned to hug his mother and then he saw the tears in her eyes. They hugged. He thought at first that it was just happiness and pride making his mother cry. Then she began. "I'm sorry. I didn't mean to spoil your day. Dear, the doctor says I have something called cancer. It can't be cured and it can't be fixed. He says I will die within a year. He says I will be lucky if I see Christmas."

Sam held his mother as she sobbed. "Do any of the others know?"

She shook her head.

"Does Dad know?"

This time she nodded affirmatively.

"Do you want me to tell everyone while we're all here together?"

At first Ann argued with him. No, she didn't want to ruin one of the first times they all-but Walter-had been together. But then Sam reminded her that this is what family is all about-that they would all be there to support her and give her their strength. They would want to do that for her and she should not deprive them of that right.

"You're right. You're such a good son, Sam. I knew I could count on you to do the right thing."

Sam thought of how many times others had relied on him to do the right thing when times were tough. "Well, we can get through this one, too," he thought, although he didn't realize then how hard it would be to watch his own mother wither and fade then have to say good-bye as she passed away in his arms.

The family was told, and each one vowed to come see her as often as possible. Like the family they were, they were true to their word. Ann was fortunate to see another Christmas. By then she was too ill to move, so the family gathered throughout the day at the home on Sunbury plantation. Sam, after spending practically all day, stopped to visit Arthur and Verna on his way home. They informed him that William had re-married a lovely woman who was an avid church-goer. They lived in Cape Charles and seemed very happy. Edward and Susan had another child, a boy this time, and lived in the big house in New York City. Paul continued to make the social rounds, still searching for "Miss Right."

Elizabeth and her husband had another son, this one named James Victor. Sam questioned where they got the name. James for his father and Victor from Victoria.

The conversation paused for a moment. Then the role call of the living commenced again. Sarah and James were expecting in February. Mary and Margaret were both happy in their marriages. They all got together often.

After Sam told them of his mother's failing condition, Arthur commented, "Yes, we have done as much for her as possible. I am sorry for your loss, but it's in the Lord's hands now."

Sam seemed to think so, too. He knew it was just a matter of time, and he promised to be back to visit again when he had the chance. He visited the cemetery before leaving, then home he went.

Ann passed away on January 2, 1909. She had said she was glad to have been a part of Christmas, even though she was too weak to get out of bed. The family gathered around her, supporting her, and drawing strength from each other. The funeral was held at Sunbury because Arthur had insisted. He also had wanted Ann buried in the family plot next to Victoria, but Javan quietly and calmly stated only once, "We have our own family cemetery, thank you." It was on the other side of the creek at Drivers, so her body was taken across in a boat after the service. The burial was simple, with only family attending.

One of the main concerns for Sam was what his father would do with his mother gone. Javan had never been one for being self-sufficient. Sam considered the options. Robert, his wife and four children were doing well on their farm, and they certainly could afford to take Javan in, but they didn't seem to want him. Richard and Mary Ann were next in line, but they were expecting another child in April. The transition might make an added burden to them. Plus, Richard didn't have extra room. His home was the apartment above the grocery store he owned in Drivers, and there was no room for expansion. Captain Charlie thought it would be a great idea for his father to come fish with him, but Sam knew how fragile his father had become. He wasn't sure he could handle being outdoors in all types of weather. That was always a possibility to keep in mind, though. Rosa and Joseph Hubbard were good about taking in all stray dogs, Sam thought to himself. "Heaven knows I've showed up on their doorstep plenty of times." But they, also, were expecting. This one was due in late February or early March. Sam thought about his three younger brothers. With Walter gone to Charleston and James and Ben courting, he couldn't picture their father living with them.

"Well, Dad," he started the conversation on the Saturday after the funeral when he had come to visit, "I have a proposal for you."

Javan, a man of few words, simply raised an eyebrow.

Sam continued, "I've done a lot of thinking about this. You see, I was used to Miss Edith being at home when I got home from work. She always had supper ready. She tended to all those little things I didn't have time for that make a house run smoothly, and she mostly was just plain good company to me in the evenings."

Sam looked at his father to see if he was following his line of logic. Javan nodded, so Sam went on, "What I'm saying is that I miss her. I miss having someone to talk to. First I lost Virdie, then I lost Edith. Not that it's the same, of course, but I miss having someone around to talk to."

Sam's words had poured out in a rush like they always did when he wasn't sure that what he was saying would be received well. He paused again, and once again his Dad nodded. Sam wished he would say something one way or the other, but as he didn't, Sam finished his thesis.

"Well, it's like this. I'm alone. You're alone. My house is paid for. I think you ought to come live with me."

Having said it, he waited for the reply. Javan didn't move at all. As if carved in stone, nothing betrayed his thoughts. After what seemed like a long time to Sam, he said, "When do I move in?"

Sam had walked up to Sunbury almost immediately after the conversation with his father. Arthur was pleased to see him, and as it was too cold to sit outside, they moved into the parlor by the fireplace. At first the two men spoke of the difficulties of the past week. Sam thanked Arthur for all the help he had been. Then Sam shared that he would soon be a train engineer with his own route. "I think one of my stops may be at Bellehaven Station," he commented. "So please share with William that perhaps I will see him over there sometime." Bellehaven Station was not too far from Cape Charles and was on the same railroad that the Brittanhaurs had used to get to New York.

Finally, Sam got to his purpose in coming. "Sir, I'm going to take my Dad to live with me in town. That way I can keep my eye on him and help him whenever he needs it. I know he hasn't actually worked for you for a while, and you've been very kind to let my parents continue to live in the house there free of rent. Thank you for all you've done for me and my family."

Arthur brushed it all aside, "You know you're like family to me. Always will be. And your family is my family. You are all good people, and it has been my pleasure if I could share some in providing a little relief or comfort."

Sam and Arthur knew that all he had done was just to live his religion. Arthur was that way. He wasn't a "go to church just on Sunday" type of man. He practiced Christian charity whenever and wherever he could. Sam knew that, but he also knew that with taking his own Dad away from Sunbury, it meant that his reasons for coming back were less.

"Sir?" he started, not knowing how to say what he felt. "I may not be back to visit for a long time. My job…and…well…"

"I know, Sam," Arthur said sadly. "We both knew this time would come sooner or later. Remember, you are always welcome here. Anytime."

They both got up and headed for the door. Sam said he intended to stop by the cemetery one more time, even though he knew the markers were covered over with snow.

"Sam, please say good-bye to Verna before you go. I know it would mean a lot to her."

So Sam did, and the older lady didn't realize that it was the final good-bye. Sam shook Arthur's hand warmly in his own and kissed Verna on the cheek with a "Thanks for everything," whispered in her ear.

Sam borrowed a wagon from Rosa and Joseph the next day. He went back to Sunbury, helped his Dad finish packing, and loaded the wagon to go. The two men stepped into the January cold with flurries drifting around their faces. They shut the door to the house that held many memories for them both. Then they turned their faces to the wind and toward town, a new phase of life starting for them both.

▼

CHAPTER 14

THE JOB

Sam and Javan fell into a comfortable routine easily. Javan was much handier around the house than Sam had imagined that he would be. He still was a man of few words, not playful and teasing like Edith, but Sam was glad to have him there when he got home after work.

Sam insisted on one thing, though. That was that Javan attend church with him on Sundays. Usually the two of them could walk the seven blocks into the downtown area. They took it easy, and Sam figured it did the old man good physically to get some exercise and spiritually to hear a sermon once a week.

Before too long, Javan asked to go to Wednesday services. Sam thought this was odd, as Javan had never been one for going to church too much. Sam told his Dad that he thought it was a great idea, but fore-warned his Dad that sometimes he might not make it back in time to walk with him to be on time for service. His route was the same every day, but sometimes it took longer than others, depending on the amount of mail to be loaded, among other things.

Sam was now the engineer of a freight train. It left from Kiptopeke each morning, stopped at Nassawadox to load freight, then on to Bellehaven station and finally to Wachapreague, the popular resort town where William and Arthur had invested money in the large hotel years before. He went past several small towns and plantations before his next stop at Modest Town. Then he crossed into Maryland and stopped at Pocomoke City. It was the largest town on his route and boasted a yard and turntable, among other things. The engine was turned and the trip back south was made after all the freight was unloaded and goods coming south were loaded on.

Javan sometimes scowled when Sam told him about his route. "You do the same thing every day. Doesn't it get tiresome?"

"Never! To feel the power of that engine under me. To be in control of that much power. Really, Dad, it's a great feeling. You ought to go on one sometime." Obviously Sam was one of the many who romanticized steam power and trains to the point of an obsession with them.

Javan just shook his head and said, "I'll stay here, thank you."

One evening Sam came home as white as a sheet. He came in the door, put down his coat and quickly sat down.

"What's the matter, son?" Javan asked.

"The train…" he asked for a drink and after downing the whole glass, he seemed sustained some, so he started again. "The train that runs the same route I do but at nighttime had an accident last night. The switch at Bellehaven Station was somehow thrown the wrong way. The engineer didn't notice in the dark, of course, and he plowed into a siding that had some coal cars sitting on it. The impact, they say, could be heard for eight miles away."

Javan sat, watching the face of his son. "Then?"

"Well, the engineer was killed and the fireman pretty badly hurt. He was thrown from the cab of the engine on impact. He was lucky the train didn't tip over on him. It just crumpled and was a terrible mess. I saw it this morning when I went by."

"I'm sorry," his father said. "Did you know the engineer?"

"No, I had never met him, what with running different shifts and all. But I had heard about him. He was supposed to be one of our best. Everyone liked him. Nice guy. Had a wife and three kids, too."

The two men sat in silence for a while, staring at the flames from the fireplace licking the air as some knot hole caused the wood to pop and spatter. Finally Javan broke the silence,

"Come home to me, son."

"I will, Sir. I will." Sam replied, knowing that was as close as his Dad got to being emotional.

As was natural, Sam made many friends with the railroad. He was an easy going, quick to learn, and mechanically capable man. That made working on the railroad easy for him. He daily had contact with his fireman and brakeman, but others who saw him frequently soon came to anticipate the shock of red hair coming toward them. Sam was always pleasant, and he never said negative things about anybody, no matter how unpleasant they were. So it came as no surprise one Friday when some of the men invited him to go out for a beer with them after work. They said they did other things together, like shoot pool and go fishing. Sam wouldn't have minded going fishing every now and then, but he wasn't keen on the idea of hanging around a beer hall and wasting time and money shooting pool. That's how he saw it-just a waste of time.

"I appreciate the offer, guys, but my Dad is waiting for me at home. He would be worried if I came home too late. But, I'll tell you, I would very much enjoy a fishing trip some Saturday."

Some of the men thought Sam was a "goodie two shoes," but others appreciated the way he put family first and himself last. Secretly, they admired his convictions. So, because he handled himself well, Sam was invited on fishing trips on Saturdays, but was left out of other activities.

It wasn't surprising to others, then, that in the fall Sam was offered another promotion. This one came as a surprise to him. He was called in to the manager's office one Friday after work. Sam never feared being called in, because he didn't have any fear of having done anything wrong. So he went in whistling.

The manager, happy to see Sam and to see him in such a good mood, began, "Sam, your good work has been noticed. We would like to offer you what we see as a promotion. It would involve an increase in pay, but it has a down side to it, also. Would you like to hear more?"

Sam smiled, "Yes, sir!"

"Well, we have a fast freight available soon when old Johnson retires. The run goes from Kiptopeke north with cars loaded with fish, seafood, and produce from the Bay Area. It's called fast freight because it is loaded with perishables and needs to get to where it's going fast. There are no stops until you reach the end of the line, which is at Delmar, a town that is partially in Delaware and partially in Maryland. At that time the train is turned around and produce that is shipped from New York and Baltimore-more perishables-are loaded and returned to Kiptopeke."

The manager stopped talking a moment to see if Sam had any questions. He didn't seem to, as he was nodding and checking the wall map to his right.

"The advantage of this run, of course, is that it pays more and is more prestigious. The disadvantage is that it takes two days. You have an overnight stay at Delmar."

Again checking Sam's reaction, the manager continued, "We figure that because you're single and young, you wouldn't mind such a run. Some of the older guys with families turn it down, even if it does pay more, simply because the rent at a place in Delmar would make them break even. We're hoping you would look at it as an adventure and an opportunity."

Sam was quiet, considering these last words. Would his father be able to take care of himself on those evenings when Sam wasn't at home? That was a concern.

"When do you need to know my answer?" Sam asked.

The manager replied, "It's Friday now. Why don't you take the weekend to think it over and let me know first thing Monday morning. Fair enough?"

"Yes, thank you. That gives me time to weigh the choices and talk it over with my father. Thank you for considering me, Sir." Sam was well known for his flawless politeness with everyone, and the manager smiled.

"Fine. See you Monday then."

Sam thought about the new job offer all the way home and wondered how he would be able to tell his Dad about this opportunity and what all it involved for both of them. Several changes would have to take place, of necessity.

Meanwhile, Javan was at home, trying to figure out how to tell his son something very important, also.

After a somewhat quiet supper, Javan and Sam retired to the parlor to sit in front of the fire, just as they did many evenings.

Javan opened the conversation. "Son, you seem extra quiet tonight. Tired?"

"No, sir, actually I have something on my mind that I wish to discuss with you."

With that start, Sam went ahead and told Javan all about the job offer. He finished with, "I'm concerned because it means you would be alone every other night, Dad. I have enjoyed your company here and I don't know if I'm ready to change that in any way."

At this, Javan cleared his throat. "Actually, son, I won't be alone."

"Well, of course you would. I would have to stay in Delmar every other night. Please try to understand…" Sam argued.

"No, son, listen to me. I've been trying to tell you something all night, also. Wednesday night at church something extraordinary happened."

Sam dreaded hearing of some spiritual awakening that his father would try to get him involved in. He had been so enthusiastic about going to church lately that Sam feared something cultish was going on, but he couldn't place his finger on it.

Javan continued. "I proposed to Defrosa McColter."

Sam's mouth dropped open. "You did what?" his voice higher than usual.

"You think I been going to church to get religion? Boy, you ought to know me better than that! Defrosa is a pretty thing, even at her age. She and I hit it off and I been meeting her at church for a long time now. Why do you think I go on Sundays and Wednesdays?"

Sam had the decency to shut his mouth, but still couldn't believe what his ears were hearing.

"I proposed and she said yes. I want to marry her, Sam. It's nice living here with you, but I miss having a female around. You know what I mean."

Sam had to admit that, yes, he did. He was shocked beyond words, so he excused himself to step outside to get some more wood for a few minutes. He looked up into the clear sky sprinkled with stars and thought, "What in the world?" But then he recognized that same yearning in himself. It wasn't the same without a woman around. And if Mrs. McColter would make his Dad happy in his old age, then he agreed to the union. He knew the lady. He knew she wouldn't try to mother him or impose where she wasn't wanted. She knew she wouldn't try to fill the shoes of his mother. She would just love his Dad and make him happy and hopefully find some happiness in the union herself.

Feeling that his head had cleared with the crisp night air, Sam went back inside. In an odd role reversal, he said, "Dad, you have my blessing. Congratulations!"

The two men shook hands, an uncommon occurrence for them, then sat comfortably in front of the fire and talked about their future plans.

On Monday, November 4, 1909, Sam began his new job as engineer of a fast freight hauling produce between Kiptopeke and Delmar. Before he accepted the job, he asked the manager where he might stay while in the latter city. The manager had told him that for the time being the station manager there had a room for let. So Sam had gone to see him the previous Saturday.

The station manager at Delmar was a pleasant man named George Barr. He had grey hair that had been blonde at one time. He was slightly pudgy and carried himself like a man who had once worked hard physically but was now glad to have an easier job.

His wife, Carrie, was a pleasant lady. She kept an immaculately clean house and was a good cook. Sam found that out early as she insisted that he at least have some pie and coffee before returning home Saturday. The apple pie was the best he had ever tasted.

The housing arrangement would be that Sam could stay in a room on the first floor near the back of the house while he was at Delmar. The room had its own door that opened onto the back yard. The rest of the downstairs was the kitchen, the dining room, the parlor, an indoor bathroom, and another room that George used as an office.

The Barr family, besides George and Carrie, consisted of a daughter, Helen, and two sons, Thomas and Edwin, although everyone called them Tom and Ed. Helen was in her last year of high school and the two boys were teenagers, younger than their sister. The family all had bedrooms in the upstairs of the square, brick house that boasted a large front porch.

Carrie, priding herself on being a good judge of character of the many engineers who had rented their room over the years, said to her husband after Sam left, "He's a good one. He'll pay his rent on time and be quiet. I expect no trouble out of this one."

George, just smiling and shaking his head at his wife's prophecy, teased, "He's young, good looking in his own way, and single. I say that spells trouble from the start."

Three Saturdays later, Javan and Defrosa were married in a quiet ceremony that was witnessed by Sam, his sister Rosa and her family, James, and Captain Charlie and his family. The other children couldn't make it for whatever reason, so Sam invited them all back to his house for a sort of reception afterward.

He served cake, coffee, and a few tidbits that Defrosa had made. She called them finger sandwiches. Sam secretly thought they were child sized portions meant to tempt a man but not enough to satisfy him no matter how many he ate. He chuckled to himself as he realized there would be a few changes in his life. Javan and Defrosa had decided to live in Sam's house. Her house was not paid for and was smaller. All things considered, it was wiser to have her move in with the men. Sam didn't mind as he knew he was going to be there only half the time anyhow, and he was pleased to not have to worry about his Dad while he was gone.

Sam's new route started early. He had to get over to Kiptopeke by 3:45 in the morning to start his run. He wasn't sure starting so early in the dark in the winter months was a great thing, but he had to admit that he did finish by 4:00 in the afternoon. This gave him plenty of time to pursue any interests he might have.

At first, Sam wasn't sure what other interests he might have. He had read everything there was to read about steam engines and trains. The library in Delmar was fairly small, so he had trouble picking a theme of study. As it turned out, he found himself being a built-in tutor for Helen.

In her senior year of high school, she was having trouble with her math and her science courses. The math, trigonometry, gave her fits. No matter how hard she tried, she couldn't figure out the difference between tangents and cosines and sines. She wailed that she would never use this stuff, anyhow, so why bother. So Sam began sitting down with her every other day while he was in Delmar. He got back to the house shortly after Helen and the boys got home from school.

That gave them time to do the minimal chores they had around the house. When Sam came, the dining room table was cleared and Sam began tutoring Helen. At first he did it out of the goodness of his heart to help her. Later he discovered that he looked forward to their time together. Once she got past the complaining about math part, she was a pleasant girl, very much like her mother.

Sam taught Helen how to use the slide rule. He told her about practical things, times when she might actually use some of the knowledge learned. He also told her how fortunate she was to have the opportunity to go to school rather than work all the time.

His lessons shed a new light on school for Helen. She had only seen it as drudgery before. Sam made her realize what a privilege it was. So her attitude changed. George and Carrie mentioned that to each other one evening after the children were in bed. Sam wasn't there that evening and he had been with them for about six weeks.

George began, "Carrie, have you noticed a change recently in Helen?"

"Yes, George, I have. And I'm not sure I like what I see," she replied.

"What?" he almost roared. "She is getting better grades in school and she has a much improved attitude about it. Before I was fearful she wouldn't finish, but now I know she will with flying colors. All because of Sam. He has turned that girl around, Carrie. Mark my words."

"Yes, George, but to what purpose?"

"What? What do you mean?" George looked puzzled.

"George, do you mean to tell me that you don't see that misty look in her eyes when Sam's around? Don't you see how Helen is suddenly transformed into a gentle, helpful, kind creature when a certain red haired man comes around? George! Wake up!"

George hadn't really fallen asleep, but he did have a glazed look in his eyes. "You wench!" he teased his wife. "You think Helen has a childhood infatuation with Sam? No! I think not. I think he just brings out the best in her, and I, for one, like her better this way!"

Carrie retorted, "Fathers are always blind about their daughters. George, I'm telling you, this is no puppy love. Helen is old enough to fall in love and she has. Head over heels in love with Sam."

There was a very long moment of silence. Then George asked in a concerned tone, "Do you think he feels the same way about her?"

"No, of course not. Right not she is his landlord's daughter who he is helping to complete high school. Nothing more. Nothing less."

George accepted Carrie's evaluation of the situation because he knew her instincts for judging people were generally correct. She had proven that many times over with all the renters who had come and gone from their little back room. But one thing bothered him, "Do you think Sam would ever...uh...I mean..."

Carried didn't want the fearful words said, either, so she replied, "No, George, I don't think Sam would ever take advantage of our daughter. I think he is an honorable man with high moral standards. I think he is a true southern gentleman. If I see any indication to the contrary, I will be sure to let you know."

With the situation in the open, the parents promised to keep their eyes open and watch for warning signs, but the next few months went on like the previous one, blissfully.

CHAPTER 15

▼

THE REALIZATION

While in Norfolk, Sam's evenings were less quiet than before. Defrosa had a little more energy and spunk to her than his father did, but the easy banter around the supper table was a welcome change. Defrosa was a decent cook and kept the house clean. But what pleased Sam the most was that his father was happy. Sometimes after coming home, they would sit in the parlor and Javan would just smile into the fire. Sam wasn't sure he had seen him smile for years, so he decided that if his Dad was happy, he was happy, although secretly Sam was a little envious of this new found pleasure in his father's life. Sometimes, as Sam lay alone in his bed at night, he wondered if he would ever find love again.

While in Delmar, Sam's evenings were very busy.

First he tutored Helen. Then the boys wanted his attention. They actually competed with each other to tell him about something they had done at school or to show him some project or paper they had completed. After supper, he spent time with George in the office area, discussing the railroad, his run, and other things in general. Sam had taken to reading about electronics and gas engines. He felt many new inventions were on the horizon. He wasn't one to invent, he told others, but he sure would like to put to good use some of the time and energy saving inventions coming out.

Sam adjusted well to living in two places at the same time. One Sunday he was talking to his Dad about getting re-married.

"Dad, do you think I'll ever get married again?" he asked, metaphorically more than anything else.

Javan, who was more straight-forward, answered wisely. "Son, some day your eyes will open and there she'll be. Like me and Defrosa. She was there all the time. I just hadn't seen her. I suspect that's how it'll be for you, too. Some gal will just pop up and all of a sudden you'll realize she had been there all along, just waiting on you to open your eyes and see her."

Sam smiled at the thought. That was about as whimsical as his Dad ever got. So he chuckled and said, "I'm sure you're right, Dad, but right now I must have blinders on, for I sure don't see any prospects."

In the Spring of 1910, Ben married a gal from Greensboro, North Carolina. She had been visiting relatives in the Norfolk area off and on for years. Whenever the whole family got together, they had a picture made, so that was how they had met. Ben had wanted her to move to the Norfolk area where he had his business established, but she had well to do family in the Greensboro area and she assured him that there was plenty of work there. So they moved.

That left James out of a job. He had been a book keeper for his brothers for so long that he had forgotten what it was like to work for anyone else. What Ben and Walt hadn't told the rest of the family, though, was that James was getting more and more ill over the years. He wasn't really able to do everything they had needed done by the time Ben left for North Carolina. So James, not knowing what else to do, showed up on Javan's doorstep one day. He had a suitcase in his hand, the extent of all his earthly possessions. Of course, Defrosa and Javan let him in and offered to let him stay. He would have to share a room with Sam, but with him being gone every other day, they didn't see that as a problem.

Sam came home to find his brother there. It wasn't a problem, as Defrosa and Javan had said, but Sam did notice the constant cough that James couldn't seem to shake. When he got a chance after supper, he took Defrosa into the kitchen and asked her about it.

"Have you noticed James' cough?" he nearly whispered.

"Yes. It's probably the consumption or tuberculosis," she seemed rather calm about either prognosis, but it upset Sam tremendously.

"Consumption? Tuberculosis? Those things are fatal, Defrosa!" he almost yelled.

"Yes, I know. Now sit down and listen to me," she seemed totally calm, so Sam did as he was told and listened to her.

"My first husband died of tuberculosis," she explained. "I did what the doctors told me was the right thing to do. I put him in a sanitarium. They said it was highly contagious. They said if I didn't do it, I would get it and would die, too. Well, I almost wish I would have died, too. Don't get me wrong, Sam. I love your father and want to take care of him, but I will never have him or one of his go through what my poor Matthew went through. He was alone when he died. The nurses there only came close to him when they had to. After I put him in there, he never felt the comfort of the human touch again. No one was allowed near except the nurses and doctor. They always wore cloths over their mouths and noses when they got near. They had special gloves they wore. I saw, though. I saw a look of sadness and longing in that man's eyes. He was alone, Sam. I deserted him when he needed me most."

Her voice had gone very quiet, but at the end of her story she rallied and said loudly, "I won't let that happen to anyone I love again. You understand me?"

"Yes, ma'am." Sam replied, knowing it was no good to argue with her about James possibly bringing disease to the rest of the household. He felt good, though, to know that his brother would be cared for in his last months and that he wouldn't be alone. That, in itself, was worth all the risk.

Sam thought about his earlier conversation with Defrosa when he was alone in bed that night, with James coughing unknowingly in a small bed on the other side of the room. "Another one of those hard decisions in life," he thought. "You do what's right and don't even worry about the rest."

Whether it was tuberculosis or consumption, the family never knew. But they watched James decline in health rapidly. He kept apologizing for being ill and for not being able to help the family financially.

One evening, only a week before James passed away, Sam got tired of hearing it.

"James, knock it off! We are family. You are here because we want you here. You're not a burden to us financially. I make good money and we're doing fine. The house is paid for. So quit feeling sorry for yourself and us and just accept things. OK?"

It was unlike Sam to be harsh like that, but he was tired of death and change. He found that more and more he desired a "normal" life. He looked at couples walking arm in arm down the street, and he wanted that. He looked at families sitting together in church, wrestling with small children to keep them still and quiet, and he wanted that. He even saw furtive glances between Javan and Defrosa that said unspoken words, and he wanted that. Maybe he was just tired and frustrated with his life. Maybe he needed a change of pace or a vacation. He didn't know which, but he knew he couldn't continue like this for much longer. So he promised himself that after James died and things settled down, he would think things through and take some action.

For the next week, James grew weaker every day, but his attitude was good. Instead of complaining and apologizing, he was thankful for every little thing anyone did for him. As a matter of fact, after Sam's outburst it seemed that he found peace with himself and his situation.

James died on the following Saturday. The illness had lingered, but his death came quickly. He started a coughing fit, not unlike many others previously, and found he couldn't get his breath at all. In a matter of four minutes, with his family standing around him and trying to help, he was gone.

The arrangements were made and the funeral was set for Monday. Only those relatives living in the Norfolk area were able to attend. The brothers closest to James emotionally and in age, Walter and Ben, both lived too far away to be able to make it. Each was sent a wire with the sad news.

Sam took the whole day off and ended up having to take off two days because of the nature of his route, but he found Defrosa disinfecting the house on Tuesday. She started vigorously cleaning everything from top to bottom, so Sam spent the day helping her as much as he could. He was actually glad when Wednesday came and he could get back to his job.

Sam reflected on that as he lay in his bed that night in Delmar. He did like his job. So, it wasn't that which needed changing. He liked his church. He even liked living in two places. OK, what else? After sorting it through, Sam decided that he would make a conscious effort to look for a wife. That was the only aspect of his life where he felt a void. Everything else he found fulfilling and worthwhile.

Along with the first of June came Helen's graduation from high school. The weekend before, while Sam was staying there, she invited him to the school for the ceremony.

"Sam, I want you to be there. You know I couldn't have made it through my senior year without you. You've been a real life saver for me and it would mean, oh, so much if you would be in the audience when I receive my diploma."

The graduation ceremony was combined with the baccalaureate ceremony because Delmar had a small graduating class. It was to be held the following Sunday afternoon. For Sam, that would mean coming up to Delmar especially for the ceremony, then taking a train back south to start his route again early Monday morning. Did he really want to do that for the wish of an eighteen year old girl? He thought about it only briefly.

"Yes, I will be there. Do you think I would miss one of the most important days in your life?" he promised her.

Helen smiled gratefully at him then unthinkingly grabbed his hand and squeezed it. "Oh, thank you, Sam! This means so much to me!" She practically squealed the last words before she jumped up and ran out of the room. Her words trailed behind her, "Oh, I have so much to do before then. What dress I should wear…"

Sam laughed to himself at her enthusiasm and then looked at his hand. His eyebrows gnarled in deep thought. What was that he had felt when she had taken his hand?

Without having to help Helen study in the evenings now, Sam found that his whole schedule at the Barr house became rearranged. When he arrived after work, he often helped the boys with whatever they were doing while Helen helped her mother fix supper. After supper, Helen was required to help wash and dry dishes, so Sam took to helping, too. His evening chat with George about the trains followed, but with plenty of daylight left, Sam wasn't ready to sit and read or go to bed. Often the family would take a walk around the town. The streets were lined with cedar trees and the houses were well kept, with well trimmed bushes placed on boundary lines and flower beds gracing the sidewalks. Sometimes they all went for a little exercise. Sometimes the boys had other plans, such as trying to meet some of the local girls. And sometimes it was just Helen and Sam. He found that he came to look forward to these times.

Having lived on a farm most of his life, he found the town of Delmar fascinating. With the summer walks, Sam came to know most everyone in town as people would either walk around or sit on their front porches to cool off in the evenings. His walks with Helen, he thought to himself, were a modern promenade.

"Good evening, Mayor Brown, how is your knee today?"

"Hello, Pastor Speight. Enjoyed your sermon Sunday."

Other such niceties transpired in infinite variations. It was kind of like a game of words, to find something nice to say to each person they met.

"Sam?" Helen began one hot July evening, "Do you ever think about getting married again?"

The two of them had walked several blocks and were on their way back to the house.

"Well, yes, as a matter of fact, I have put a lot of thought into that subject recently," he replied honestly.

"What would you like in a wife?" Helen asked.

Sam had to think. Women could be so blunt, he thought. He hadn't stopped to think about requirements in a wife like a shopping list. It wasn't like he would go to the grocers and ask for 110 pounds of meat, nicely dressed, etc. How was he supposed to answer this crazy question?

He stuttered at first, "I'm....not...sure."

"Well, what's important to you?" she pressured. "Church going?"

Yes, he would have to admit that was very important.

Helen pursued the matter, "Good cook?"

Not necessarily, but it would be a plus.

"Energetic?"

Yes, but not too much so. He didn't want someone who would run circles around him and would tire him out just watching her. He wanted a woman who worked hard while he was working and knew when to just sit and talk in front of the fire.

That was fair. Now Helen felt that they were starting to get somewhere. "Pretty?"

Well, yes, that would be a definite plus, also. Sam knew he sounded vain, but he preferred someone without red hair, he told her.

"What age?" she asked bluntly.

"I reckon it doesn't matter much," he said thoughtfully. "I don't want someone so old that she can't get around, but I guess that doesn't matter so much at my age as it does at yours, Helen."

By now they were in front of the house. They paused. Helen seemed to want to ask him something else before they got within ear shot of the rest of the family.

"Sam?" she started with a tremble in her voice. "Would you consider marrying someone like me?"

What did she mean "someone like her?"

"I don't know, Helen," he said truthfully. "I hadn't thought about it."

"Oh, well, good night, Sam." She hurried off as if she had forgotten something, running straight up to her room.

Carrie looked up from her chair where she was reading part of the local paper when Sam came in.

"Sam, is Helen alright?" she asked.

"Yes, ma'am, I think so," he answered, also puzzled. "She was asking me some odd questions and I think I didn't answer the way she thought I would. I'm sorry if I upset her."

"Don't worry about it. I'll check on her later," Carrie said, going back to her newspaper.

Sam didn't get much sleep that night. He kept re-playing the conversation with Helen in his head. She had an annoying way of cutting straight to the quick, he thought. But then he softened. She was right, though, what did he want in a wife? He decided to make a conscious effort to figure that out. Maybe that's why he hadn't found one yet. Maybe he wasn't catching any fish because he hadn't gone fishing.

Carrie also didn't get much sleep that night. After finishing the paper, she had gone upstairs to check on Helen. Always having had a good relationship with her daughter, she knocked lightly on the closed door to her bedroom, then gently opened it and peaked inside. She spied her daughter, face down on her bed, crying.

"Helen, for mercy's sake. What's the matter, dear?" Carrie held her daughter to her as she cried.

"Mother, Sam doesn't even know I exist!" Helen sobbed.

"Well, of course he does, dear," she comforted. "He came out of his way to attend your graduation, right? And he takes you on walks in the evenings now." Then her mother stopped, the realization of what her daughter was really saying caved in on her.

"Helen, don't tell me! You're in love with Sam!"

Helen sobbed all the more into her mother's shoulder.

Carrie closed her eyes and wondered how to handle this. She had known from the day a daughter was born to her that they would some day face this sort of problem, but she was hoping she still had some time before that day came. Well, today it would be, then. She gathered her strength, said a quick prayer for guidance, and said, "Honey, if he's the one for you, then he will have to discover that for himself. All the beguiling and flattering on your part won't change a thing. My advice is to sit back and wait and see."

Helen stopped sobbing to listen, so Carrie continued. "He lives with us every other day. If he can't see what a fine young lady you are, then that's his loss. Right?"

Helen smiled. Her mother always knew the right words to say.

"Thank you, mother," she sighed, wiping her tears. "You're right. Please don't tell Daddy I've acted so foolishly."

Carrie and George had a lot to talk about that night before they went to sleep.

Sam seemed unusually quiet the following night when he got home to Norfolk. Defrosa caught him in the kitchen long after supper. He was after a simple drink of water and he almost dropped the glass when she interrupted his reverie.

"Alright. What's up with you?"

"What do you mean? Nothing's up," Sam replied, knowing it wasn't completely true.

"Something happened over the weekend that has you bothered. It's something you can't get straight in your head. Now out with it before you burst, young man."

Sam laughed. "You're a challenge to have around," he said fondly to the older lady. Then he poured out his heart to her. After he was done, she took her chin off her hand where it had been resting and said, "So when will you marry Helen?"

"What? I hadn't given any thought to…" Sam stopped. "So that's what this is all about. She thinks that I…that she…oh, brother."

The realization of what Helen's conversation was all about came upon him. Defrosa had made him see that Helen wasn't speaking in generalities. Helen was wondering what there was about herself that he didn't like. Helen was in love with him.

Sam held his head in his hands, wondering why he hadn't seen it before. Now everything was so clear to him. The furtive glances, the time spent together, the walks, the talks, the graduation ceremony. Feeling like he'd been hit with a carload of bricks head-on, he asked Defrosa, "So what do I do now? How do I go back to Delmar and pretend nothing ever happened?"

"First of all," she replied. "Nothing has happened. Secondly, you need to decide. Would she make a good wife for you? I know she's a lot younger, but is that really a factor? Finally, what would be wrong with you marrying her? It's not a sin, you know."

With that, she patted him on the shoulder and said, "It's late. I'm off to bed."

Sam looked at his watch, the same one Edith had given him years before. "Oh, my goodness! Yes, it is late. I've got to get some sleep."

Sam went to his room, but he knew sleep wasn't going to come until he had thought through and sorted out this situation a little more. By the time the alarm went off for him to get to work, his decision was made.

Sam cautiously approached George's office room after supper that evening. Although it was part of their routine, Sam felt uneasy this time.

"Sir, may I shut the door today?" Sam asked as he came in.

George looked up from the pile of papers on his desk, including papers and reports from all over the Eastern Shore. "Yes, Sam, if that makes you more comfortable."

Sam wasn't sure how to begin, but George seemed to be in no hurry. So he started with, "I have enjoyed living with your family very much, sir, and I feel very much at home here."

George nodded, foreseeing where this was going, but not wanting to make it any easier on Sam.

"You and your wife have been very good to me, Sir, and I can't thank you enough."

George interjected, "You pay your rent on time and you're a handy person to have around. You worked a miracle with Helen and her schooling."

"Uh, yes, Helen," Sam was stuttering now. "That's what I want to talk to you about, sir."

George nodded for him to continue.

"I…I mean…she…I mean…we," Sam started and couldn't seem to come up with the right words. He looked up and George was smiling with obvious enjoyment.

"Go on," George said.

"I'd like to have your permission to have your daughter's hand in marriage, sir." Sam rushed through the words as if he didn't say them right then he never would.

George laughed, came around the side of the desk, and slapped Sam on the back. "I officially welcome you as a valid member of this family. Congratulations, Sam!"

Sam was overwhelmed. No arguing about differences in age. No discussion of Sam's previous marriage. No talk of "be a good husband to her, she's my only daughter, you know." Sam sat down before he fell down.

"That's it? You don't mind? I mean…" Sam found himself stuttering again.

George relieved the pressure. "Sam, Carrie told me the other evening about Helen's conversation with you. After that, it was obvious that she was in love with you. When you're not here, she whines and pines and tries our patience to no end. When you're here she is bright, bubbly, responsible, and even interesting. You bring out the best in her. Carrie and I only hope that she will bring out the best in you and make you very happy."

The wedding was planned for late in August because the Barr's had relatives who lived at quite a distance who they were sure would want to come. Invitations were sent out. Carrie and Helen spent their days sewing and planning. Sam and George continued their business, as usual. The two boys tried to stay out of the way and out of trouble.

When Sam was there, he and Helen took their usual walks in the evening around town, but now everything had a new look to it. Sam felt his heart and step were light. Now he tried his best to remember all the names and faces associated with the odd little town of Delmar. If it was going to be his home, he wanted to know everyone and have everyone know him.

The wedding turned out to be a large church event. The whole town turned out, it seemed, and the day was stifling hot. Sam smiled as he met relatives from Baltimore and Chincoteague and Salisbury and even Washington, D.C. He thought his face may never be the same shape again by the end of the ordeal.

After the wedding, Sam and Helen took the train to Wachapreague. They had reservations at the resort hotel there for three days. Sam was looking forward to his honeymoon, but was a little fearful that he might meet William there. "No," he thought, "he rarely checks on his investments. So what are the odds? Besides, I think the last I heard was that he re-married. It would be awkward, but if he can, so can I." With his conscious eased and his new bride at his side, he stepped on board a passenger train heading south for his honeymoon.

Helen had never been outside Delmar before, so she marveled at the plantations. Several famous ones from that area caught her eye. Covington, Windingdale, and the Kerr Place. Each was spectacular in its own way. Tobacco fields. Sweet potato fields. Corn fields. Each held her interest until the next came into view.

They also had a spectacular view of the ocean from their fourth floor window at the Wachapregue Hotel. The resort hotel boasted an elegant lobby with a huge crystal chandelier and sweeping staircases. The Otis elevator could have entertained Helen for hours, Sam thought, smiling at the fresh and enthusiastic way she saw each new thing. For Sam, it was like re-living his youth. Everything was fresh, new, and exciting. He smiled at his young bride and hoped she would always retain her youthful enthusiasm.

All too soon their three days were finished. The arrangements had been made for them to live at her parent's house until they found something suitable on their own. By the time they got back, the bigger bed from Helen's room replaced the twin bed from Sam's room.

Their lives fell into an easy routine. By day, Helen spent more time with her mother, paying attention to all those things that help make a household run smoothly. Now she showed intense interest in shopping, gardening, cooking, cleaning, and doing the laundry. Her mother was well pleased with the progress her daughter was making.

"If I had known you were going to be this helpful after getting married, I would have married you off years ago!" Carrie teased her daughter.

The evenings when Sam was in town, he and Helen spent a lot of time walking around town. Now not only did they greet all the neighbors and speak to each, they scoured the town looking for a home of their own.

CHAPTER 16

▼

THE ROUTINE

By Christmas of that year, Sam and Helen had found a place to live. It was a small house behind one of the local stores on Main Street. It wasn't great, but it afforded more privacy than they had living with Helen's parents.

Christmas Day was spent with her parents, then Sam treated Helen to another train trip. The following Friday night, after work, he cleaned up and they took the southbound passenger train to Norfolk. Helen had packed a suitcase for them, which included a change of clothes and small gifts for Javan and Defrosa. They arrived fairly late, so they pretty much had greetings then went to bed. Saturday was spent visiting with Javan and Defrosa. The couples exchanged gifts and had a wonderful meal together. Sunday found Sam taking Helen to church. He wanted to show off his new bride, but he also wanted to establish the routine in his family that Sunday was a day of rest and time to worship God. After a quick meal at home, Sam and Helen were headed north again.

Defrosa had promised a shopping trip into Norfolk for Helen, but time did not permit this time. Helen enthusiastically reminded Defrosa of it before they left, and the two women said they would get together soon. Javan was glad to see that they got along so well.

The year 1911 came in with no special events either positive or negative. Sam and Helen had settled into a comfortable routine. They often spent Sunday afternoons with the Barrs after church. Sam and Helen were living well, with no financial worries. They would have liked to have a larger home, but it wasn't necessary, Sam said, until the children started coming along.

The whole year seemed fairly uneventful. Sam liked it that way. In fact, he preferred it that way. He felt, in retrospection, that he had enough excitement in his earlier years. He was content to work and spend time with his family now.

They did make a trip to Norfolk at Easter time. This time Sam took a day off so that Defrosa and Helen could have an extra day for shopping. Both ladies bought themselves a new outfit that would be suitable for church or a nice outing. Helen also bought some new shoes for Sam and some new curtains for their house. Sam didn't mind that she didn't make them. Helen wasn't as talented in domestic arts as other women that he knew, but he knew he made enough money that it didn't matter.

For their first year anniversary, they returned to Hotel Wachapregue for a weekend. They both felt that it was an exhilarating experience that refreshed and renewed them. The weather was pleasant then and the walks that they took along the beach were a time to be together, just the two of them, and not have to think about anything.

1912 came in much the same way. Sam reflected that the years seemed to be passing by quicker as he aged. He recalled from his childhood how a year seemed to take forever. Now he blinked and another one was gone. While staying up to see the New Year in, he asked Helen,

"What do you wish to be different this year than last year?"

She looked at him carefully, as if almost afraid to say what was really in her heart. Finally, she licked her lips and said, "We've been married nearly a year and a half. This year I would like to have something that's missing from our lives."

"What's that?" Sam asked.

"A baby," she said quietly.

Sam had been so busy with his job and so content with his travels that he hadn't stopped to think that Helen might feel lonely during the days while he was gone. He stopped to think. Yes, it was odd that she hadn't conceived after that long, but he remembered that it had taken a while for Virdie to get pregnant also.

"Well, what do you say we just keep practicing?" he asked in a playful way.

"I guess that would be a good way to start a new year," she responded, just as playful. So off to bed they went.

Sam tried not to compare his life with Helen to his life with Virdie. Helen suited him fine. She never aggravated him or nagged him about things the way some of the men on the railroad complained that their wives did. When he got home at night, she was waiting. She had herself clean and looking nice. The house was tidy. The chores that she could do were all done. She usually had a meal ready. Her cooking was acceptable and she was continually improving. In the evening they would walk around town when the weather was nice or sit near a coal stove in the living room when it was cool. Their conversations were easy and pleasant. There was no animosity or uneasiness between them. And yet, something was missing.

Sam didn't feel the burning protectiveness like he did with Virdie. He and Helen didn't tease and joke around as much as he and Virdie had done. They didn't have private inside jokes. They didn't just sit to listen to the birds. Maybe he was older and less romantic. Sam took all the blame upon himself. He knew Helen was happy, although she longed openly and fervently for a baby. Maybe this gnawing inside him was just an attitude. He should be happy. Life had never been easier. He enjoyed his job. He had no financial problems. He had friends and plenty of people around him to spice up conversation. He still had his railroad friends he could go fishing with whenever he wanted. So what was the matter? He knew something was, but he couldn't put his finger on it. "Don't dwell on it." he thought. "It will only make you more unhappy."

Again for their anniversary they went to the beach. This time, while walking along the beach, Helen was obsessed with all the families with children. She seemed to notice nothing else. Sam tried to turn her attention to the trees, the birds, and the fresh air. He even took her fishing in a boat. All she could talk about was what a great father he would make some day and how he would be able to share all his knowledge with a son.

Sam was actually glad to go back to work the following Monday. She didn't realize that she was being obsessive, he was sure. But the pressure was becoming greater. Even people they knew, like their pastor in Delmar and Helen's parents, began to ask questions that sometimes made Helen cry after they were home alone.

Sam found that he went fishing more often, usually going with his fireman. Virgil Hearn was a pleasant man of 22. He had no family. He was from the Baltimore area and had run away from home as soon as he could at age 15. He'd been on his own for years, and what he liked most was working on the train. Sam felt a kindred spirit with him from the start concerning that. Often the two men would go to the James River that was near Delmar and spend a quiet Saturday. Sam knew this meant more time away from Helen and more time that she was left alone, but he felt that if he didn't get out and talk to someone, he would shrivel up and die.

He and Virgil could talk about anything. Virgil was one of those soft-spoken people who you knew would keep a confidence. Sam didn't mind telling him about his problems. He also knew that Virgil was non-judgmental. It didn't matter to him what another person did, said, or thought, as long as it didn't affect him.

"Shoot," he said one time, "My aunt is married to a Negro. My oldest sister is not married and has two kids, each by a different guy. My Dad is an alcoholic. Does that make you think any less of me?"

Sam admitted honestly that it didn't. "No, Virgil. You're you. You're hard working, likeable, and that's all there is to that."

"Right. So, what's the problem?"

Sam smiled and was glad that he was blessed with good friends.

The holidays were spent the same as the year before. Sam and Helen were finding it difficult to figure out what to get each other. She liked to shop for store bought things. He appreciated home made things. She liked store bought things. Sam preferred to make things with his hands. "Like I did the oak cradle," he thought. In retrospection, those were some of the happiest days of his life.

So 1913 came. Sam suggested that Helen do some volunteer work. Perhaps working with the Women's Circle at church, in the library, or at the school could help stimulate her mind and take it off the fact that they were thus far barren. She considered this for a while.

"I don't think being around kids all day will improve my attitude any," she commented. "So the school's out. Besides, you know I wasn't the best scholar anyhow."

Then she thought about the church. "I don't sew well. What do I have to offer those ladies?"

Sam tried to imagine what a Women's Circle did. "You have a lot to offer. Fresh ideas. Young blood. You could run errands for the elderly ladies who can't do things for themselves any more. You can write letters to missionaries overseas. I don't know what else because I don't know what else they do. But you have lots of talents. Just use one."

His last statement came out harsher than it was intended. He meant for it to be a compliment, but it sounded like a criticism about laziness.

"Well, I never!" Helen stormed out of the room.

Perhaps the holidays were just more difficult. Some people said they were. While he waited for her to cool off, Sam polished his shoes and put Neatsfoot on his leather belt. Keeping himself busy and his mind occupied was a survival strategy he had learned long ago.

March 11, 1913 started out like any other day. Sam arrived at the station in Chiptopeke as always. He went through the routine safety check with his brakeman and then his fireman. Nothing seemed out of the ordinary, until he spotted a movement out of the corner of his eye just as he was climbing up into the cab.

"Just a minute," he told Virgil. "I thought I saw something."

"Well hurry up, man," his fireman said. "It's time to go!"

Sam jumped down and went around the engine to the other side. He walked quietly to where the first two cars were coupled together. There, climbing up between the two, was a Negro man of about 35 years of age.

"Hey, you there!" Sam shouted. "Come down this moment!"

The man stood up on top of the first car. He shouted back. "Look, I'm just trying to get to Salisbury. My family there and my little one be sick. I work in Norfolk and I just be trying to get to my little one. That all. Let me ride."

"No, I'm sorry," Sam said. "It's against all regulations. You've got to get down. A passenger train comes by here in about an hour and a half. You can ride that."

The man tried to argue with Sam, but Sam held his ground. "I'm sorry, man, but now. I can't wait any longer."

The man reluctantly climbed down, muttering something under his breath.

Sam thought about asking him what he said, but he was already behind schedule, so he ignored him and ran back up to the cab, jumped in, and took off for all he was worth.

The night of March 12 found Sam staying overnight at The Bird's Nest. He had told his father about his worries. "Am I just being ridiculous?" he asked his Dad.

"No, son, I know what you mean," he began. "You should know that I love Defrosa very much, but she knows it's not the same love as I had for your mother. Your mother is the woman who bore my children. She's the one who saw me through some pretty bad times-times when I didn't make any money-times when I wasn't much of a husband or father. Yet she stuck by me. I grew to love her more each day, not because love naturally is that way, but because of the depth of what I saw in her that she saw in me. Each day she grew more dear to me. Not because of anything in particular or anything big. It was because of those little things, like steadfastness, faithfulness, kindness, and gentleness. I didn't love her because she was a good cook or a good romp under the covers. I loved her because she was herself.

I can appreciate those same things about Defrosa. I can appreciate her cooking, cleaning, doing my laundry, running errands, and doing a hundred things a day that make my life easier. I can appreciate waking up next to a warm body. But it's so much different. It's not less and it's not more. It's just different."

Sam looked at his watch and noticed it was very late. "Thanks, Dad. I think I feel better, but I'm not sure what I'm going to do."

"It's OK, son. Sometimes we just have to go along with life. The high spots and the low spots come, but life's better when it's just routine, trust me!"

That monologue from Javan gave Sam a lot to think about. He lay in bed that night thinking that he wasn't really unhappy. But, on the other hand, he wasn't really happy, either. When the alarm went off, he wasn't sure he had slept at all. Usually he could make decisions after thinking them through, and that was that. But not this time. This time he felt like he was no closer to sorting out his problem than he had been the day before, the week before, or even the month before.

Perhaps it was because he was tired from lack of sleep. Perhaps it was because his mind was preoccupied with figuring out what to do about his relationship with Helen. Perhaps it was just one of those things that happens that is supposed to happen and nobody ever knows why.

Sam went through the routine safety check that morning. Everything seemed in perfect condition. He pulled the engine away from the station and picked up speed. The newspaper account tells best what happened next.

"Died in train accident. Story goes that Sam had kicked off a Negro riding illegally. This black man got off and turned the switch on the train thus causing the train to derail. Buried in Delmar, DL with large grave stone. Sam and Virdie's wedding performed by Arthur B. Sharp. 1901 he was a farmer. In 1880, listed as a step son of 9/12 yr. Living with in-laws George M. Barr in 1910 in Wicomico Co., Md. near the state line in Delmar, Del. The lot in Delmar, Del. where he is buried was purchased by his father in law, George M. Barr (1860 1917) on March 19, 1913, on the date of Sam's death." (Paraphrase written by Charles T. Harrell)

News release for the Accomack News, March 22, 1913, page 1. "Train Wrecked, Engineer killed and Fireman Injured" Engine no. 13 with what is known as D.2, a fast freight in tow was derailed just opposite Belle Haven Station at about 4 o'clock Wednesday morning, instantly killing the engineer, Mr. Samuel Harrell, of Bird's Nest, Va., and supposedly fatally injuring the fireman, together with totally demolishing four freight cars and their cargoes, while the engine appears to be a total wreck. The supposition is that some one tampered with the switch lock that caused the engine to run off the track, as it was badly battered when examined. A singular incidence is that the same engine had almost the identical fate about four years ago in less than a quarter of a mile where this wreck occurred, at that time killing both its engineer and fireman."

News release for Peninsula Enterprise, March 22, 1913, page 3, col. 3. Same as above.

News release for The Sun, Baltimore, March 20, 1913, page 1, col. 5. "Two Killed in Collision, Fast Freight Runs Into Open Switch Near Cape Charles." Cape Charles, Va., March 19. Samuel B. Harrell, engineer, was killed and Virgil H. Hearn fatally injured at 4:25 o'clock this morning when a fast freight train on the New York, Philadelphia and Norfolk railroad ran into an open switch at Bellehaven Station. The injured man died several hours later in the Norfolk Hospital where he was taken for treatment. Both men lived at Delmar, Del. The engineer dashed into a switch upon which were six cars loaded with cinders. The engine and five cars were demolished and eight others derailed. The lock to the switch was broken and thrown away, and the railroad officials express the belief that it was a deliberate attempt to wreck the train.

News release for the Baltimore American, March 20, 1913, page 1, col. 4. "Train Wreckers Kill Two, Switch on the N.Y., P. and N. Had Been Tampered With." Special Dispatch to The American. Cape Charles, Va., March 19 At 4:25 o'clock this morning No. 1, a fast freight train on the New York, Philadelphia and Norfolk Railroad, at Bellehaven Station ran into an open switch leading into a siding on which were six cars loaded with cinders, demolishing the engine and five cars and derailing eight more. Samuel B. Harrell, engineer, was instantly killed, and Fireman Virgil H. Hearn so seriously injured he died in the Norfolk Hospital a few hours later, where he was taken for treatment. Both men resided at Delmar, Del. It is quite evident that the party or parties who tampered with the switch did so with intent to wreck a train. The lock to the switch was broken and thrown away. Trains had been passing over the switch during the night in perfect safety.

Bellehaven is on the Virginia Eastern Shore in Accomack Co., near the Northampton Co. border.

CHAPTER 17

▼

THE LESSON

George Santayana (1863-1952) said, "Those who cannot remember the past are condemned to repeat it." As Charles T. Harrell researched his ancestors, he found striking similarities between their lives and his. He thought about the life of his great-uncle. He thought about his grandfather and father, both who had since passed on. He wondered if other people felt the burning desire that he did to discover those people from the past whose names we see on gravestones and to know more about them. He wasn't content with just a birth and death date. He wanted to know how they felt about things and what kind of personalities they had. He wondered if people a hundred or two hundred years from now would want to know about him. Would anyone remember the details, or even the generalities, of his life? Or would he be like the Harrell whose tombstone read, "Gone, but not forgotten," but nobody knew how that person fit in with the family. They all figured he must somehow as the surname isn't a very common one and the gravesite was near known relatives. But being content with the sketchy parts wasn't enough. So throughout the next few years, Charlie spent much time and energy searching for more. More details. More newspaper clippings. More connections. Unable to find more information about what happened to Helen, he has had to content himself with the fact that he may never know everything he would like to know, but this book has given Sam a place in history that he deserves and he will not be forgotten.

Notes

Having never written a historical fiction novel previously, I don't mind telling the readers that this is my first attempt. The idea came when my husband, in the summer of 2000, decided to sojourn to the Delmar area to take our son, Javan, to the grave site of "Uncle Sam." A six year old was not impressed, but a 43 year old was. It seems that this story, as I state in the first chapter, has been handed down in the Harrell family for years, nobody really knowing what was the absolute truth. So we began to do the research. I must also tell you that this book didn't turn out the way Charles or I thought it would. Sometimes the characters would wake me at 2:00 a.m. and want me to write more. (This happened right before the two main characters were married.) At other times they wouldn't let me write. (This happened right before the main female character's mother dies.) I know it sounds odd, but the fictional characters took on lives of their own. They haunted me, in a friendly sort of way.

Now, for the accurate historians among the readers, let me delineate what is real and what is fiction. Isn't there a place for both in our lives? If not, step aside Brothers Grimm and Isaac Asimov. Also, some events are fictional. But, like the people, they seem likely to me.

Real people & events

The entire Harrell family (although nieces and nephews are omitted)
Virdie (Victoria)
George and Carrie Barr
Virgil Hearn
Defrosa McColter
Walt's accident

The train accident
Captain Charlie being a fisherman

Fictional people & events

Virdie's parents, brothers, their spouses, and their children
Arthur, Verna, their girls, the girls' spouses and children
Frank (foreman at Sunbury)
Edith Taliaferro and her son
The preacher and his wife
The Barr sons
The eels incident
Sam living with Edith
Richard's grocery business
Javan living with Sam

For those of you who want to know the real story, instead of the historical fiction that combined bits and pieces of personalities of my own, Charles, my Dad, and several other people I know, the facts as we currently know them are presented in a database called Family Tree Maker. If anyone would like more information on the Harrell family or tangents thereof, please contact us at the following e-mail address. harrellc1@verizon.net

978-0-595-38121-0
0-595-38121-9

Printed in the United States
42558LVS00003B/562-588